SWEAR YOU WON'T TELL?

Vedashree Khambete-Sharma is an award-winning ad-woman in her mid-thirties, which is okay because mid-thirties is the new mid-forties. Or something. For the past twelve years, she has peddled everything from moisturisers to magazines, like some kind of one-woman corner shop. Before that, she was a freelance reporter for several newspapers and wrote on a wide range of subjects from student suicides to types of boyfriends. Yes, that's right. Throw in a middle-class Maharashtrian upbringing, a convent education and an English literature degree, and you get, well, confused mostly. But also, inspired to tell the stories nobody else is telling.

She lives in Mumbai with her husband, daughter and the niggling feeling that she has forgotten something.

This is her second book.

SWEAR YOU WON'T TELL?

VEDASHREE KHAMBETE-SHARMA

HARPER
BLACK
An Imprint of HarperCollins *Publishers*

First published in India in 2018 by HarperBlack
An imprint of HarperCollins *Publishers*

Building 10, Tower A, 4th Floor, DLF Cyber City, Phase II,
Gurugram Haryana – 122002, India
www.harpercollins.co.in

2 4 6 8 10 9 7 5 3 1

P-ISBN: 978-93-5277-672-6
E-ISBN: 978-93-5277-673-3

Typeset in 11/14.2 Warnock Pro at
Manipal Digital Systems, Manipal

Printed and bound at
MicroPrints India, New Delhi

To Arjun and Irawati,
without whom this book and this life
would've been infinitely less interesting.

Oranges and lemons sold for a penny
All the schoolgirls are so many
The grass is green and the rose is red
Remember me when I am dead.

– English nursery rhyme

Prologue

The corridor outside the morgue smelled of phenyl. A sharp acrid smell that left even those who had never smelled it before, feeling distinctly uncomfortable without quite knowing why.

The body in the corridor smelled of Mahim Creek in all its fetid glory. Someone had thrown a dirty cloth over it, but a quick look beneath revealed that the corpse wasn't very old. Early thirties, if you were the type to play guessing games with dead bodies. So, not old, but in another sense, yes, definitely old. The sea and its children had had some time to do their work on it. So much so that you could barely make out whether a man or a woman lay beneath the sodden scraps of yellow jersey and blue denim. But pull them apart slightly and you could tell the saltwater-bleached corpse was female.

The harsh fluorescent light fell on a bloated hand protruding from under the cloth that mercifully covered the rest of the body. Rigor mortis had set in and the fingers were stiff. The fingernails still showed traces of pink nail polish. A fly had settled on the index finger, drawn by the smell of decay. Ward boys and nurses passed by, muttering to themselves. That was understandable.

The corpse reeked. It was gruesome. It was unbearable.

It was *perfect.*

One

The conference room ceiling had thirteen little cracks in the plaster. Fifteen, if you counted the squiggly ones next to the fan. There was also something greenish up there that could be moss or just the remnants of the infamous Pesto Pasta Incident. After ten minutes of staring at it, Avantika Pandit turned her gaze back to her colleague.

'Um-hmm,' she said.

It was the prelude to the weekly editorial meeting, that little time before Nathan Alvares, the editor, walked in, and for reasons beyond her understanding, this was when people felt compelled to share bits of their personal lives with each other. The person currently engaging in this exercise was Shibani Rao, *The Mumbai Daily*'s Arts and Culture correspondent.

A petite bundle of tiny clothes and industrial quantities of mascara, she was a ticker tape of random information about herself that she assumed people would find fascinating. Quite mistakenly so, in this case. So far, Avantika had pointedly yawned, stretched, stared at the ceiling, the floor and her watch; had basically hinted in every polite way possible that she couldn't be less interested in Shibani's monologue about the 'mad crazy place I went to on Friday night.' She should've known better. Shibani in weekend discussion mode wouldn't take a hint even if it masqueraded as an all-expenses paid trip to Tahiti, or wherever all the cool kids were going this year.

Avantika wished Uday would hurry up. Uday Desai was one of the few people at *The Mumbai Daily* that she got along with. Come to think of it, he was one of the few people she'd got along with in journalism school too. Now, he was equal parts friend, confidante and drinking buddy and it was he who had told her of the job opening here. She was beginning to suspect that it was his idea of a really elaborate prank. True, she needed the job after *Belle* magazine had shut down. But, she thought wryly, she should've known how amazing it would all turn out, especially since Nathan had made her feel ever so welcome.

'Look,' he'd said in his bored monotone, 'I need a reporter and your CV is the only one without a typo. So yes, you're hired. But this isn't some fancy-schmancy magazine. I don't need any airy-fairy types here.'

Luckily for Avantika, neither of those words applied to her. So she'd joined the following Monday and had quickly discovered that as far as job profiles went, the only difference between writing for *Belle* and writing for this newspaper was how glossy, or not, her words looked in print. Now, wondering if Shibani would shut up if she shoved a handy cement mixer into her mouth, she looked at the clock on the conference room wall. It was ten past eleven. Not only was Nathan late, an event by itself, but so was Uday. At which point she saw him strolling into the room.

Uday never walked. He sauntered. He looked like a fresh-faced twenty-year old and took life at an easy pace; uncommon traits in a reporter, especially one on the wrong side of thirty. But behind the baby face and lazy gait was a mind so sharp you could probably dice tomatoes with it. Today, he had a kid with him. A teenager, by the look of it. Fresh out of college, if at all. The skinny joggers, the Captain America t-shirt were all promising signs, although the look of near-terminal enthusiasm was unexpected. Avantika straightened up and smiled in anticipation.

Uday eased into the chair on her left and Avantika took the opportunity to turn away from Shibani, who was now babbling about some organic yoga cafe she'd been to, where they probably served spiritual enlightenment in jam jars.

'New trainee,' he said, indicating the boy.

'Hi, I'm Wayne,' the boy said holding out his hand.

'Avantika,' she replied, shaking his hand. 'There's a mirror in the men's room.'

Uday rolled his eyes and patted the bewildered Wayne on his back.

'V-A-I-N,' he said, 'Wordplay.' Turning to Avantika he said, 'Really?'

She shrugged.

'So Wayne,' she said. 'You want to be a reporter?'

'Yes ma'am,' he replied. 'I'm passionate about the truth. I think people deserve to hear it.'

She raised her eyebrows.

'What truth?'

'Sorry?'

'What truth do you mean?' she repeated. 'The earth is round, EDM is just noise, crying babies on airplanes are the most effective ad for contraception—what truth?'

Wayne looked abashed for a moment.

'Um ... the truth. You know, in general.'

She stared at him, then looked at Uday, who looked away. At first she thought it was because he was trying not to laugh, but as she followed his gaze she realized Nathan had walked into the room.

Avantika often thought the editor of *The Mumbai Daily* looked more like someone's nondescript uncle than the editor of a popular newspaper. Thin, balding and middle-aged, he'd be in a room whole minutes before you realized he was there, and his facial expressions often had nothing to do with his actual mood. Now, blank-faced as ever, he slipped into the chair at the head of the table and started the meeting.

'Reuters says there was another blast in Gaza,' one of the features editors at the table announced.

'Near the Pyramids?' gasped a shocked voice.

In the stunned silence, everybody turned to look at the culprit. It turned out to be Wayne, who promptly went pink in the ears.

'That's Giza,' said Avantika, 'in Egypt. Whole different continent, genius.'

Uday kicked her under the table. She ignored him.

'Give him a break,' Nathan drawled. 'He's new.'

'To what? Geography?' she laughed.

This time Uday's kick was harder. It didn't hit her hard, but what did was the fact that nobody else had even cracked a smile. She looked around quizzically. Everyone was studiously avoiding her gaze, as though she was standing outside a railway station handing out pamphlets offering a break into Bollywood, no previous experience required, just call this number and ask for Munna. Nathan, on the other hand, looked her right in the eyes. And smiled.

'Uday can do Gaza,' he said pleasantly. 'You, Avantika, can cover this.' He passed a sheet of paper to her and without a second look her way, continued the meeting.

Avantika skimmed it: it was an invitation to a press conference for some designer. It was exactly the kind of thing she used to cover at *Belle*. Exactly the kind of thing she had hoped to avoid, as Nathan well knew. She opened her mouth to say something when Uday's elbow nudged her gently. He passed her a scrap of notepaper. It had one word in his neat, cursive hand: *Nephew*.

Avantika closed her eyes and swore. Way to go, Pandit. With a sigh, she began reading the details of the invitation and stopped dead at a name in the first paragraph.

Aisha Juneja.

Damn it. Please let there be more than one of those. She did a furtive search on her phone for 'Aisha Juneja designer'. The images it threw up were of the same person and also, because this was the internet, of random women in various states of undress. She ignored those and focused on the one that looked familiar. She wore her hair short these days. But the mocking grey eyes, the imperious mouth and the bored expression were exactly as Avantika remembered. She sighed. She would have to get out of this event somehow. Perhaps, she could fall ill on the day. Or butter up Uday into covering it for her, or even Shibani. But no, Nathan would find out and she was still on probation. Stop it, she told herself, it's not an exam. Just talk to Nathan and sort it out. What's the worst he can do? One, bite my head off in public, two, fire me, three, bite my head off in public and *then* fire me.

Nevertheless, after the meeting, she followed Nathan into his office. He was sitting on his roomy swivel chair, reading the Reuters report. The wall behind him was full of large framed black-and-white photographs, some from the stories he'd broken over time, others taken years ago, at Press Club functions. In some of the photographs, you could see a younger Nathan, a man with an intact hairline and a mouth that could still turn up at the corners without a trace of sarcasm.

She knocked on the door. He looked up.

'What do you want?' Before she could answer, he continued. 'Let me guess, you want me to send someone else for that press conference.'

'Yes, because—'

'... you're too good for it.'

'Ye- no. Actually—'

'You're a smartass, Pandit. This is a newspaper, not a comedy club. You're doing this thing. End of story. Now, out.'

'Nathan, give me anything else. Please! Anything! I don't want to go there! Seriously, *anything* else!'

Nathan leaned back in his chair and peered at her over the rim of his big, black square-framed glasses. 'Stop being so dramatic. I'm not sending you to review *Housefull 6*.'

'It's ... that designer and I ... we were ... at school together.'

'Schoolmates, huh?'

Avantika grimaced.

'No. Definitely not.'

Nathan nodded sympathetically. Then he grinned and said, 'Too bad.'

Avantika frowned at him and stomped out of the cabin. She was just out of the door, when she heard him say, 'Oh, and take Wayne along. He's never been to a press conference before.'

Uday was reading up on the specifics of the Gaza incident, when he heard the chair behind him creak. There was a loud sigh. He ignored it. Another sigh, then some muttering. Uday turned around.

'He said no.' It wasn't a question.

'Yes! The bastard!' Avantika fumed, 'I offered to cover *anything* else in exchange, but the man just *refused*!'

Uday waited. He could sense it coming.

'I told him why as well, it's not like I'm being snooty, there's a genuine reason I don't want to go there!'

Any minute now.

'And to top it all, he wants me to take Wayne "What Is An Atlas" Trainee with me! Do I look like a babysitter? Do I?'

Wait for it, wait for it.

'So listen ... do you think you could um—'

And there it was.

'No, Avanti, I don't think I could um.'

'You don't even know what I was going to say!'

He gave her a bored grin.

'Could I cover it instead? Could I talk to him? Could I tell him you got run over by a taxi? Doesn't matter. I'm not doing it.'

Avantika was torn. She had already finished wheedling once since morning. Twice would be far too much to inflict on her own ego. But she really, really didn't want to see Aisha Juneja in the flesh again. Just the idea of it made her skin feel all hot and itchy like that summer when she had broken out into a rash and had to practically bathe with Caladryl every day.

She gave it one last shot.

'Uday,' she said.

'Yes?'

'You remember I got my wisdom tooth removed last month?'

'Yes?'

'You remember how they had to stitch my cheek to my jaw?'

'I still don't believe that happened.'

'You remember how the wound got infected and they had to drill around and do it all over again?'

He squirmed in revulsion. 'You just like bringing this shit up, no?'

'This press conference is going to be more painful than that.'

He laughed and shook his head.

'Avanti, you're a grown-ass woman. Stop being so scared of a damned meet-and-greet.'

Avantika drew herself up with as much dignity as she could muster. 'I'm not *scared* of it. I just don't want to do it. It's like reading Paulo Coelho. Or making a jodi.com profile.'

'Aha, and how's *that* going?'

Avantika waved her hands vaguely. Rishi had been two years ago. Now, she was a thirty-two-year-old single woman, a creature considered dangerous and possibly defective by Indian social norms. You couldn't let unmarried women run amok, in case that kind of thing caught on.

Elderly aunties with nothing better to do had started hounding her mother about matrimonial procrastination, till the poor woman had buckled and made a profile on an arranged marriage website[1]. Just because one boy turned out to be ... unsuitable ... it didn't mean there weren't other fish in the sea, her mother had reasoned. Avantika had gently asked her to back off as the whole experience had put her off marine life for a while.

These days, her father made a habit of logging on to the profile when she was around and sighing pointedly at all the eligible bachelors out there just going to waste.

Now she tried her luck one last time.

'Are you going to help me or not?'

But Uday was already getting up, glaring at his phone.

---

1 To the naked eye, matrimonial sites are like non-alcoholic beer—they both seem to take something fun and interesting and remove all possibility of it leading to sex. But lust always finds a way. So while parents think enrolling on a matrimonial site can allow their darling son or daughter to get to know a prospective spouse, they often have no idea that the young people in question are also getting to know each other, well, biblically.

'Can't,' he said. 'Got to write the Gaza story. Also, I'd rather eat a dictionary than cover a fashion event. You're on your own,' and because he knew she hated it, he added, 'Babe.'

Avantika watched him leave. According to her watch, it was already 2 p.m. If she left now, she could make it to the Taj ballroom in time for the press conference. Maybe she could slip in unnoticed. And it's not like she had to meet Aisha in person or anything. She'd be in and out like a shot. It would be painful, but quick. Like an express bikini wax.

Oddly enough, her stomach rumbled at this point. She hoped they'd serve some decent food at the place. It was the Taj, after all. Cheering up a bit at the prospect of five-star snacks, she grabbed her helmet and her black leather satchel. She was about to head to the door, when she heard someone yell her name.

'Avantika ma'am! Ma'am!' Wayne was running to her, his backpack flying behind him.

Damn. She'd almost forgotten about him.

'Just Avantika,' she said. 'Let's go.'

'So what happens in a press conference?' Wayne asked.

They were waiting at the Marine Lines traffic signal on Avantika's scooter. A red Honda Activa that behaved itself on most days and made it unnecessary to offer her firstborn child to taxi drivers in exchange for a ride to work every morning. Now, sitting astride it in the rider's seat, with Wayne perched precariously behind her, she stared at the sea through the visor of the helmet. The sun, was being its usual democratic self, shining with equal indifference on the backs of luxury sedans and taxis, on the hair of couples necking on the Marine Drive promenade, and on the tin cups held out by the urchins pestering them for coins. A balmy breeze from the Arabian Sea blew her hair against her face, a brief respite from the sweat trickling down her neck.

It was a hot afternoon and the helmet[2] made it worse. But that was Mumbai for you. You wouldn't get anything done if you sat around complaining about the heat. Plus, she was trying to be patient, she really was, but this idiot child was getting on her nerves.

Was I this daft when I started out, she wondered. Did my seniors want to whack me on the head too? She swallowed the impulse to wreak violence on a minor, turned her head towards him a bit and answered his question.

'People speak, we ask questions if we want to, daydream if we don't, they give us press releases and freebies, sometimes food, then we go back to office and write fifty words about it. A hundred, if there's a celebrity.'

It wasn't, strictly speaking, the perfect description, but what did he know? He thought Gaza was filled with pyramids.

'Sorry if I, you know, pissed you off or something.'

Avantika rolled her eyes. She must've sounded harsher than she felt.

---

2 In Mumbai's hot and humid weather, helmets are to bikers what underpants are to toddlers. They know they've been told to wear one, they know they'll get into trouble if they don't wear one, but left to their own devices, they'll take it off the first chance they get.

'No, it's not you, I'm just ... it's not you, okay?' she said, mentally adding, 'Even though it's your fault I have to go for this thing.'

The traffic light turned green, saving her from a longer explanation, and they sped off towards the Taj Mahal Palace hotel.

An enduring landmark, rumoured to have been the result of a stunning architectural gaffe[3], the Taj stands for old money, old world charm and since 26 November 2008, for terror tourism. History has it that the hotel was built by Jamshedji Tata, after he was denied entry into the then-fancy Watson Hotel. The charge? He was, at the time, suffering from a serious case of being born brown. Whatever its origin story, today the Taj throws its doors open to all of humanity—white, black and brown. Well, at least to that section of humanity that draws six-figure salaries. And to the section that included people like Avantika—journalists and other media professionals who got invited to the high-brow events that were hosted at the Taj.

As she made her way inside, Wayne tagging behind her like a wide-eyed wheeled suitcase, Avantika paused to wonder at the ambience. The hushed tones, the rich

3 It is commonly believed that the architects who designed the structure screwed up the plans and so the hotel was built with its backside facing the sea. It's not true. Although interestingly enough, thousands of Mumbai citizens find themselves in the same position every morning, without any assistance from architects whatsoever.

but subdued music, the tasteful decor littered with odd pieces of art; the Taj was not very different from any other five-star hotel in Mumbai. But it was elevated in the mind's eye because the mind came from a middle-class to which the Taj, was THE TAJ. You were going to THE TAJ. Better wipe your soles properly on the doormat. Are you wearing good, clean underwear? What if you crash into a waiter and fall into a pile of diamonds and die? Then *everyone* will know you were wearing tatty underwear to THE TAJ.

The press conference was in the North Crystal Room, all ornate carved pillars and nineteenth century chandeliers. The doors were closed, but there was a PR lackey sitting at the table outside. Avantika glanced at her watch, 3.45 p.m. They were late. Just as well, she thought as she signed for both of them and picked up their press passes. With any luck, nobody would see her get in. Or out.

The room was dark, but in the light of the audio-visual presentation playing on the large screen at the back, she could see people huddled over tables. She made her way to the nearest empty seat and sat down. A second later, there was a thud and a muffled yelp. Amidst whispers of 'Ssshhh' and 'Quiet!', Wayne got back to his feet and slipped into the seat next to her.

'I tripped over the—' he began, but she cut him off with a 'Ssshhh.'

On the screen, blank-faced, pouty models held Aisha's new Spring-Summer collection of handbags, as a breathy female voice extolled their virtues. Bold neons, soft pastels, and vibrant floral prints had been moulded into reasonably attractive shapes. Avantika could see why terminally fashion-conscious bloggers had christened Aisha the 'hot new designer on the block'. But for the life of her, she couldn't imagine why anyone would want to shell out the thousands of rupees each of these bags cost. Then again, it wasn't like she fit the consumer profile for these things. All *her* handbags were bought from Dharavi[4].

She stifled a yawn and hoped that the AV and the conference would end soon. It's not often that the Universe actually listens to your inner monologue, but perhaps in this case it did. Because just a few seconds later, the AV ended and the lights came on. A plump woman in a lavender skirt-suit came on to the makeshift stage, and began essentially repeating everything the AV had said about the collection.

'Is that the designer?' Wayne whispered.

Avantika shook her head and scanned the crowd. 'That's her, there, next to the tall guy in the glasses.'

Wayne turned in the direction she was pointing at.

'She's hot,' he said with awe.

Avantika didn't bother glaring at him. It would take too long to explain to this boy that nobody asked for his knee-jerk reaction to the looks of a woman he didn't even know. And, also, because it was true.

---

4 What *Slumdog Millionaire* conveniently forgot to mention in its poor-India-exotic-India photo essay, is that Dharavi is also home to dozens of leather boutiques, which sell everything from Mulberry knock-offs to made-to-order jackets, at a fraction of the original price. You're welcome.

It takes a special kind of person to carry off black jodhpurs, a fitted black waistcoat minus a shirt, a silver lamé bow-tie and matching silver trainers[5]—the kind of person who only feels at home under a spotlight, the bigger and brighter, the better.

Now, as the plump woman on the stage made way for Aisha, Avantika found herself marvelling at her. Here was a woman in a pixie haircut and an outfit that was part horse jockey, part male stripper, who was nevertheless oozing the kind of electric self-assurance that makes men go weak in the knees and women go wild with jealousy. It wasn't fair. It didn't even seem like she was trying, as she graciously answered a question from a *Vogue* correspondent.

'Same old Aisha,' she muttered.

'You know her or what?' Wayne asked.

Clearly, her mutters weren't as quiet as she'd thought. Kicking herself mentally, she nodded.

'Same class in school.'

'Oh, really?' asked a jolly female voice.

The plump woman who had introduced Aisha, had materialized behind her, holding a bottle of mineral water in her hand. Before she could respond, the woman held out her hand.

'Hi, I'm Renuka from Glitz PR.'

'Avantika Pandit, *Mumbai Daily*,' Avantika said. 'And that's Wayne,' she added as an afterthought.

'Nice to meet you, you know Aisha from St Agnes?'

'St *Agatha*.'

---

5 A.k.a designers. Also, stylists. Also people who don't mind being mocked to death in college.

Renuka smiled smoothly and for some reason, Avantika felt as if she'd already known that. 'St Agatha, of course, silly me, would you like to meet her, it could be easily arranged,' Renuka said. She was clearly a woman with no time for question marks. Or full stops.

For one mad moment, Avantika considered telling her that Saint Agatha may not be available for a meeting, what with her having died some eight hundred years after Christ.

'Erm, no thanks, we must get going. Lots of work at office.'

'Nonsense, I'm sure you can steal ten minutes—'

And before she knew it, Renuka had grabbed Wayne by the arm and frogmarched him towards the stage. Avantika considered leaving at this point. Then she imagined Nathan's face when she would have to tell him that some random PR valkyrie had taken his Precioussss away at the press conference, while she legged it from there. She sighed. Some days you were just a hydrant for the Universe to piss on.

Dragging her feet, she followed Renuka and Wayne to the front of the room. The tables at the back were mostly occupied by the sorts who had come here just to fill column space. But the front of the room was a different story. The clothes were quirkier here, the handbags much more expensive. Here were the journalists who weren't just interested in fashion, but often, dictated it. The style editors of *Cosmopolitan* and *Vogue,* the hosts of TV shows dedicated to fashion and the ten most popular fashion bloggers in India. These were the ladies who could tell a Birkin from a Kelley, knew what the next 'It' bag was going to be and could make or break a designer with a mere fifty words of print. They were, in other words, the Handbag Mafia.

They were all currently staring at Wayne, whose Adam's apple was bobbing up and down like a contestant on *So You Think You Can Dance*. Renuka was introducing him to Aisha. Avantika almost pitied him at this point, but she pitied herself more.

'And he's come with a friend of yours from school,' Renuka trilled. 'Avantika, from *Mumbai Daily* ... right, dear?'

Avantika stepped forward with a nod. Her body language had changed in the last second or so, to completely conceal the distaste she was feeling. 'Yep,' she said with a smile. 'Hello, Aisha.'

It was worth it, just to see the look of horror on Aisha's face. The next second, it was gone and her grey eyes narrowed.

'Hello,' she said, in tones of chipped ice. 'Long time.'

'Yes,' Avantika agreed, 'long time.'

1989

There was a parrot on the tree outside the window. It was eating something Avantika couldn't see. Probably a guava, she decided. The parrot in her storybook ate a guava. And a red chilli. But the thing in the parrot's beak wasn't red. Or chilli-shaped. It was green and white. So it was probably a guava. The mystery satisfactorily resolved, she turned her attention back to class. It was English period, her favourite. She liked all the new words and writing with pencils and

Miss D'Sa, who reminded her of her Aunty Rujuta. She liked everything about being in the first standard actually. The small recess and the big recess and the bells at the end of the periods and her classroom with its white walls and her wooden desk and wooden bench painted blue, and all the lovely notebooks and pencils.

Ooh, and she loved her uniform. She had never worn a uniform until she came into primary school. And then, one day Aai and Baba had taken her to a big shop and bought her three! She looked at the one she was wearing now. It was so smart, a pink and white checked shirt, a dark pink pinafore and a pink and white checked belt. She lovingly smoothed her pinafore, feeling the soft fabric under her fingers.

'Can I come in, Miss?'

A girl was standing at the door. She looked old. Probably in the third or fourth standard, Avantika thought.

'Not "can", Kashmira, say "may I come in",' corrected Miss D'Sa.

'May I come in, Miss?' the girl called Kashmira said.

'Yes, you may.'

'Miss, Miss Francis has called you to the 3B classroom, Miss.'

'Now?'

'Yes Miss.'

Miss D'Sa sighed. Then she looked at the class and said, 'I'll be right back, everyone. Don't make a noise, okay?'

'Yesmiss!' the class chorused.

'Just copy what I've written on the blackboard.'

'Yesmiss!'

'I don't want anyone to tell me that the class was talking when I wasn't here.'

'Yesmiss!'

Satisfied, Miss D'Sa followed Kashmira out of the class.

It was at this point that Avantika realized with sudden horror, that she needed to go to the bathroom. Really badly. But how? Miss D'Sa wasn't in class. She couldn't leave the classroom without taking permission from Miss D'Sa. It was not allowed. Oh, how she wished she had asked for permission instead of staring at the parrot!

She looked around nervously. Everyone was busy copying the sentences Miss D'Sa had written on the board. Everyone, except Mitali, who sat in the next row and was always being yelled at by Miss for not doing her homework. Maybe if she held on for some time, Miss D'Sa would come back and then she could ask for permission and go to the bathroom.

So she turned her attention to her notebook and started scribbling. A few minutes later, her bench partner turned to her and said, 'I finished. You finished?'

Avantika shook her head. Miss D'Sa had told them not to talk.

'Why you are writing so slowly?' the girl asked.

'Sssh, Miss said no talking,' Avantika whispered.

The girl giggled. 'But Miss is not here to see who's talking, no? And no one will tell her, because she only said she doesn't want anyone to tell her the class was talking.'

Avantika glanced at the door, worried. Miss *had* said that. But it still felt ... wrong.

'Let me write,' she said instead, and picked up the pencil.

'Then write,' her partner said, but there was an odd smile on her face.

A moment later, Avantika felt a finger tickle her neck. She turned around and whispered, 'Stop it!'

'No,' her partner giggled, tickling her again, this time on the side of her waist.

'Stop no, please!' Avantika said with a whine.

But it didn't stop. Avantika wriggled and squirmed, her body tense and her mind full of fear, till she couldn't take it anymore.

'Stop it no, please!' she cried, 'I feel like going to the bathroom!'

Her partner stopped the onslaught immediately. 'Really?' she asked, her face serious.

'Yes,' Avantika replied, relaxing.

And then, to her shock, her partner grinned and started tickling her again, only much, much harder. She tried controlling herself, she really did, but it was no use. She felt her underpants get wet, and a thin trickle flowed down her legs, wetting her uniform. Her nice new uniform.

Avantika felt her eyes sting and before she knew it her face had scrunched up and she was weeping great big blobs of tears. Her nose, clearly feeling that her eyes shouldn't be doing this alone, joined in and began to run. Avantika covered her face with her palms and cried and cried, trying to drown out the whispers and giggles as more and more girls saw what was happening and joined in.

Then a gentle voice in front of her said, 'Girlie, girlie[6], take this.'

---

6 It's unclear who invented this form of address in Indian convent schools. One can only hope that the person is engaged in a life-and-death fight with sharks at the moment.

Avantika peeped from behind her hands. The girl sitting on the bench in front of her had turned around and was holding a hanky.

'Don't cry,' she said. 'If you cry, they'll tease you more.'

Avantika took the hanky. It was pink and had an L embroidered on a corner, with a pattern of roses. It was so pretty. She didn't feel like making it dirty. The girl seemed to understand that.

'It's okay,' she said. 'You can wash it and bring it tomorrow.'

'Thank you,' said Avantika, sniffling and wiping her face.

Then she folded the hanky and placed it carefully in her pocket.

'What's your name?' she asked the girl.

'Laxmi Swaminathan,' the girl replied.

Avantika wanted to say thank you again, but suddenly, the whispers and giggles died down. There was what Miss Francis often called 'pin-drop silence'. Miss D'sa was standing at the door, a stern expression on her face.

'Why are you all making such a noise?' she asked. 'This whole class is going to be punished now.'

'Miss, miss,' a girl from the third row said, putting up her hand. 'That girlie did susu in class, Miss!'

The whole class giggled. Avantika felt her eyes sting again, but she remembered what Laxmi had said, and she didn't cry.

Miss D'sa looked shocked. 'Who?' she asked, her threats of punishment forgotten, 'Who has gone to the bathroom in the class?'

Miserably, Avantika raised her hand.

'Very bad, Avantika, why didn't you go to the bathroom to ... go to the bathroom?'

Avantika stood up, shaking. 'M … miss, you weren't h … here m … Miss … how … to—?'

Miss D'Sa looked confused. She took a deep breath. 'Come with me,' she said.

Avantika followed wretchedly, the back of her wet pinafore clinging to her thighs. She could feel the eyes of the whole class on her, as Miss D'Sa led her out of the classroom. She had no idea where she was being taken. What if she got punished? What if they told her to not come from tomorrow? She liked school, she didn't want to stay at home. And what if Miss D'Sa took her to Miss Francis and Miss Francis gave her a note in her diary? Mitali was getting notes all the time and one day Miss Francis had even called her parents to school! What if Aai and Baba were called to school to meet Miss Francis? Her eyes filled up again and she wiped them away with the back of her hand.

But Miss D'sa didn't take her to Miss Francis's room, which was on the second floor. Instead, she took her to the first floor, to the staff room. Avantika had never been inside the staff room before. It had big windows and tables and chairs and dark grey steel cupboards. When Avantika entered with Miss D'Sa, two other teachers were sitting at one of the tables. One teacher, whom she didn't know, was correcting notebooks with a red pen. The other teacher was Mrs Cama, her craft teacher. Avantika liked her. She had a soft voice and always smiled in class.

As Miss D'Sa came in with Avantika, Mrs Cama looked up from the magazine she was reading. She saw the patch on Avantika's pinafore and smiled.

'Spilled water on your uniform, dear?' she asked.

'No Miss ... I ... I did—'

'She went to the bathroom in class,' Miss D'Sa said briskly, opening one of the steel cupboards and taking out a neatly folded spare uniform and clean white cotton bloomers.

'It's alright, dear,' Mrs Cama said in her soft voice. 'It happens.'

Avantika cheered up a little at that and felt just a little less nervous, as she went with Miss D'Sa to the toilet to change.

She was back in class, twenty minutes later, her uniform, underwear and eyes, all dry. Her bench, on the other hand, was still wet. She raised her hand.

'Miss, bench is wet, Miss.'

Miss D'Sa, who seemed to want this period to end almost as badly as Avantika did, gave her a tight smile.

'Then sit next to Laxmi, till peon-dada cleans up.'

For the first time in the past half hour, Avantika felt like smiling. She picked up her schoolbag and went and sat next to Laxmi, who promptly shifted along the bench and made place for her. But she didn't have time to feel happy for too long. The period was almost over. Once the bell rang for the next class, Miss D'Sa would rub off the blackboard. Sitting down, Avantika hurriedly started copying the sentences on the board in and managed to copy them all before the bell rang.

As Miss D'Sa left the class, her old partner nudged her in the ribs and began singing, 'Susu girl, susu girl!'

Avantika turned around angrily. 'I only did it because you tickled me! Say sorry!'

'No,' said the girl, and made a face.

'Say sorry! You're supposed to say sorry when you do a bad thing!'

'No! I won't!'

Avantika clenched her fists. She had never felt so angry before. When you did something wrong, you were supposed to say sorry! And this girl was not saying sorry! And there was *nothing* she could do about it! She felt her eyes sting again, but this time out of sheer rage. She felt like hitting someone. No, she felt like hitting a very specific someone.

Just then, Laxmi spoke up. 'Just say sorry,' she told the girl calmly. 'Or I'll tell your name to Miss, okay?'

The girl glared at Laxmi as if she was a strange new kind of beetle.

'I'm not doing anything to you, no? Then why you will tell her my name?' she asked.

'Because you're not being nice,' said Laxmi. 'Just say sorry, okay?'

The girl glared at them both, her eyes filled with loathing.

'Sorry,' she said through clenched teeth.

Avantika's fists slowly unclenched and she breathed out. She knew what she was supposed to say next. She was supposed to say 'it's okay'. She was supposed to forgive. Good people always forgave others, even if they weren't nice to them, Miss Francis had said that day in assembly. God loves those who forgive, she had said. But Avantika was still angry. So she said the worst thing she could think of, something she had never said to anybody else ever, ever.

'You're a bad girl, Aisha. I hate you.'

Two

'And then, Kaira introduced me to this guy, Nico? He used to work in a circus in Romania, no wait, I think he's *from* Romania and *worked* in a circus someplace? I'no ... anyway we went out for drinks to Big Nasty? And ermagawd, we were there till like the place shut down? But then Nico didn't want to go home? So then I said—'

Avantika mentally retraced the conversation, as Shibani went on. Let's see, she had finished her coffee and was writing up the press conference and Shibani had waltzed up to her desk and said, 'Guess what I did last night?' and ... yes, that's it. She had said it. She hadn't been paying attention and she had said the word. What. She had said, 'What?' No, she had only herself to blame.

But hey, she told herself, at least the press conference was over. She had met Aisha in the flesh and she didn't have to go through *that* for at least the next two thousand years, give or take. Compared to that, Shibani's auditory ambush was like a persistent housefly—irritating, but largely ignorable. And speaking of irritating—

She smiled sweetly at Shibani and said, 'That sounds *fascinating*, Shib. You know who's really into that kind of stuff? Uday.'

Shibani blinked. 'Uday's into fusion haiku?'

'Totally,' said Avantika. 'Just yesterday, he was saying how much he likes to ... erm ... fuse haiku ... with ... erm—'

'Slam poetry?'

'Slam poetry, yes,' she finished, ignoring the urgent cries of her brain for an explanation. 'Why don't you go and tell him all about it?' she added.

As Shibani bounded away, miniskirt swishing against her thighs, Avantika sat back, satisfied. Maybe this day wasn't going to be a total—

'Pandit! Get in here!' Nathan's voice cut through her optimism.

She pursed her lips and with a resigned sigh, plodded over to his cabin. Nathan, seated in his usual spot, peered at her over the rim of his glasses and asked, 'How was it?'

'*Fun*, I guess,' she replied, packing as much sarcasm into the three words as she could.

'Good. Then you'll love this. Your friend Aisha's,' he smiled at her grimace, 'PR team thinks it would be great if you interview her. For the weekend supplement.'

Avantika's mouth opened in horror. 'What! Why?'

'A lifestyle piece. How she got into the field, what inspires her, her favourite designers, blah blah, you know the drill.'

'B ... but why *me*?'

'Because you're buddies from school and all. Renuka seemed to think it was sweet.'

'Renu-! Why does she get to decide this? Can't you send Shibani? This is exactly the kind of crap she likes!'

'Yes, but I don't want to ... disappoint Renuka. Especially since she's so generously offered me VIP passes to the Mumbai Indians match on Saturday.'

'So you're just going to ... you *know* ... Jesus! This is so...' she fumbled around for words but sometimes the English language is just woefully inadequate. She took a deep breath and forced herself to calm down. This was ridiculous. She was a professional. If Nathan wanted to make her life miserable, well, he'd have to do a lot worse than send her for an interview. With Aisha. Jesus fucking aaaaargh!

'When? When is this ... thing?'

'Apparently Aisha is travelling next week, so it has to be tomorrow morning. Eleven sharp. Normally she'd have met you at some coffee shop, but Renuka said since you guys are friends, you can go over to her place. It's at—'

'... Pedder Road, I know.'

'Been there, done that, huh?'

'Yes,' Avantika snapped, 'Also bought a t-shirt that says "Never want to be there again"!' And with that she swept out of his cabin. The effect was somewhat spoilt by Wayne who crashed into her at the door.

Avantika's hands had curled into fists and it was taking every ounce of her self-control to not whack Wayne, who was mumbling terrified apologies. She took a step back and was about to walk past, when she heard Nathan ask, 'Wayne, you want to see how an interview is done?'

Avantika spun around. 'You do that and I quit,' she said, pointing a finger at Nathan, who laughed.

'In this job market? I don't think so.'

'Why, why are you doing this to me?' she asked, aghast.

Nathan thought for a moment. 'I don't know,' he said. 'Maybe because it's *fun, I guess*.'

What does he have against me, she asked herself for the hundredth time. She had asked Uday the same question yesterday after walking out of Nathan's office, and even he had seemed at a loss. Sure, she didn't always think before cracking a joke, she *could* be more diplomatic, but surely neither of these was a punishable offence. And this interview *would* be a punishment. Sitting there in Aisha's living room, asking her brain-dead questions and worst of all, being subjected to that stare the whole time—that stare that said, can we get this over with, loser?—her teeth clenched just thinking of it. She needed something to take her mind away from it all. Luckily, riding a scooter through Mumbai traffic offered enough of a distraction.

She got off the Western Express Highway at Mahim, shooting a now-mandatory glance at the Bandra–Worli Sea Link[1]—a cable-stayed bridge over five and a half kilometres long that offered a wonderful view of the Arabian sea and the Mumbai skyline. Had two-wheelers been allowed on it, the bridge would've brought her to South Mumbai, SoBo, or as it was generally referred to, 'town'.

1 When grammatically confused students ask, 'What is irony?' they are told that the answer is the Bandra–Worli Sea Link. It is possibly the only stretch of road in the city empty enough to test the mythical fourth gear of your car. It is also a place where you can cannot, by law, drive over 60 kmph. This is why Delhi laughs at Mumbai.

She often wondered about that. 'Town', as opposed to 'countryside'. Apt really, for an area that contained, among other things, the city's art district, most of its British-era architecture, most of its heritage sites, some of its most popular educational institutions, and last, but not the least, most of its old money.

A reasonable amount of which lived in the area Avantika was about to enter. Breach Candy, Altamount Road, Pedder Road, Carmichael Road—names from a time when Mumbai was still Bombay and Bombay ended at Dadar. This was a land of posh apartment buildings, parks, charming bungalows and Antilla[2].

As Avantika's scooter left the Haji Ali Dargah behind, standing serene and distant in the middle of the sea, she marvelled at how little the place had changed. Well, it had in some ways. A new mall, where Crossroads used to be. The onslaught of coffee and fast-food chains, some local, some American. And the roads had changed, of course. There were more traffic snarls now than before. Ditto for potholes. Even now, construction work was going on to repair the especially huge ones on Pedder Road, before the rains began in June. Considering it was already May, this was an endeavour that treaded the fine line between optimism and delusion. Traffic was being rerouted from

---

2 Opinion is divided on the famous Ambani residence. There are those who declare Antilla an eyesore, and there are those who require an urgent appointment with the optometrist. And then there are those who say, with an enigmatic smile, that perhaps the greatest luxury unimaginable wealth offered you, was the luxury of not having to look pretty.

the Mahalaxmi temple signal. She'd have to go all the way around Breach Candy and double-back to get to Aisha's house. But it didn't matter because look! Here was Amarsons and Premsons, here was Snowman's with its chocolate softies and black forest ice-cream cakes, here was that place where she'd had her first ever Frankie[3]—it all came back to her in a rush, pages of memory flying so fast and furious that for a moment, she almost forgot to breathe. And then, before she knew it, she was there. Bungalow 67: Ellora.

Black iron gates. Impeccable white walls colonized by armies of white bougainvillea. A two-storeyed bungalow surrounded by a profusion of green. Frangipani and laburnum, towered over a lush green lawn, bathed in sunlight and shadow. She had loved it from the moment she'd first seen it and she realized with a pang that the years hadn't changed the way she felt about it. Or how sad it made her. Sad, because she didn't seem to have any distant relatives willing to leave her a fortune so that she could buy a place like this. Still, a girl could hope. She parked her scooter outside the gate with a sigh and showed her press card to the security guard who had come around to shoo her away. She waited as he informed someone in the house

---

3 Kolkata might brag about its Kathi Roll, but if greasy street food is what you seek, you cannot ignore the Frankie. A refined flour paratha fried in questionable oil, stuffed with nameless stuffing, it is nevertheless a triumph in mindful eating. In the sense that your mind is so full of the taste, you don't mind the fact that you're not eating anything even remotely healthy.

of her arrival through an intercom, and walked in after he waved her on.

Ding-dong. No new-fangled buzzers or tasteless chirps for this house. The door was opened by a housekeeper who showed her into the drawing room. As she sat on the colonial-style teakwood sofa, something caught her eye. It was a large black and white photograph of the seafront outside the Taj. It seemed as if the photographer had stood right in the middle of a flock of pigeons as they took flight. The Gateway of India peeped out from amidst the flurry of feathers and wings, against a sky full of dark thunderclouds.

Avantika walked over to look at it closely. It really was quite stunning. The birds in mid-flight, some so sharply in focus, you felt you could almost reach out and touch them. And the Gateway, so often the centre of every photograph that tried to capture Mumbai, relegated to the background, almost as an afterthought. It seemed as if—

'Can I help you?'

A man was standing behind her, with a look of polite curiosity on a face that was, she had to admit, quite easy on the eyes. Mid-thirties, she decided, taking in the slight greying at the temples. Works out, too. She suddenly, irrationally, wished she was wearing something more interesting than skinny jeans and a fitted top. She unconsciously pushed back her hair, which the helmet had helpfully plastered over her forehead. Who was this? Aisha's husband? Boyfriend? Or … oh, wait. This was him, wasn't it? The brother. Oh, dear God.

'Hi, Avantika Pandit,' she said, holding out a hand, 'I'm here to interview Aisha for the Mumbai Daily.'

He shook her hand, with a smile. He had dimples.

'Dhruv, I'm Aisha's brother—'

'I know.' It came out, just like that.

'Sorry?'

She kicked herself mentally. It's like she had no control over her mouth these days.

'Um ... Aisha and I were in the same class at school. I'd ... uh ... come over for a ... party ... once?' Good God, that sounded *awful.*

'Oh,' he said. 'Well, nice to meet you again. Would you like something to drink? Coffee? Tea?'

'Thanks, I'm good,' she replied.

'I'll just tell Aisha you're here,' he said, just as she turned to look at the photograph again. 'You like that one,' he said, with a smile.

'It's fabulous,' she said. 'Who's the photographer?'

'Me,' he said simply and then added, 'on a good day.'

She smiled politely. She always got the impression that modest people were faking it. As if under all the self-effacement they were going, 'Behold! Cower, mere mortal, before my mighty genius!' She didn't see the point of it. May as well say a nice thank you and move on.

'I hope you have more good days then,' she said.

He grinned and left and she returned to the photographs and the postcolonial grandeur of the room. Teak and rosewood tables littered the place, with knick-knacks that probably cost more than the entire location budget of a Bollywood movie. One piece stood out amongst the expensive odds and ends. It was a framed photograph of three teenagers at a party. A grinning young Aisha, long hair falling to her waist, stood with her arms thrown around two others—a younger Dhruv, with a messy 90s haircut and acne and another girl, once a familiar face, now long-forgotten. Laxmi Swaminathan peered out of the photograph, her dark eyes serious, her hair pulled back in a long, thick plait. Avantika turned away from the picture, just in time to see Dhruv enter the room. He looked a little upset.

'I'm sorry but Aisha's been called away on an emergency. Perhaps you can reschedule your interview for some other time?'

Avantika stared at him. She should've expected this from Aisha. An emergency. Yeah. Right.

'No problem,' she said with a forced smile. 'Hope it's nothing serious. Like a runaway clutch. Or a tassel explosion.'

To her surprise, Dhruv sighed.

'I know what it sounds like,' he said in a dull voice, 'but it really is serious. Her best friend went missing a few days ago and they've just found her ... body.'

There are times when you're gliding down a staircase in high heels, when you think you're pulling it off, being all Grace Kelley-like, and then you trip over your own treacherous feet and fall flat on your face. That had never actually happened to Avantika, but she now knew exactly what it would feel like, if it did.

'Oh...' she began.

'Actually ... you were in Aisha's class, right? Did you know Laxmi?'

He may have said something else after that. But Avantika had stopped listening.

Three

Avantika got on to the scooter and started it, not quite focusing on what she was doing. Laxmi. Dead. No. Her mind refused to compute the information. She veered out of Napean Sea Road, honking mercilessly at anyone foolish enough to cross her path. Laxmi was dead. No. She couldn't be. What difference does it make to your life, a part of her—probably the left brain—asked. It's not like you were best friends anymore. You weren't even friends. You didn't even know she was missing.

It was true. She hadn't really thought of Laxmi all these years, except in passing—on seeing a similar-looking stranger on the road, perhaps, or while passing by their school on her scooter. She hadn't even looked her up on Facebook. And yet, Laxmi was the first real friend she'd had, the first friend who had stayed a friend through most of school. Still, her left brain insisted, it doesn't make any sense, you feeling so worked up about it. Oh shut up, she told it. And ignoring every rational impulse to drive straight to the *Mumbai Daily* office at Kalina, she took a right turn towards Girgaon. They wouldn't expect her back in office for some time. She had to find out what had happened.

Laxmi's house was a modest two bedroom-hall-kitchen apartment in the by-lanes of Girgaon. It had been a quiet neighbourhood back in the day, and Avantika felt oddly relieved to see that it hadn't changed all that much. She had no idea how many times she had visited the place. Most evenings after school, she'd stop by on the way to the Maths tuition class she attended with Laxmi. And of course, all those Saturday afternoons when they had worked on projects together, fuelled by Laxmi's mom's delicious home-cooked lunches. As she climbed up the old-fashioned staircase to the first floor, for the first time she wondered if Laxmi's family still lived there.

The nameplate still said Swaminathan. But that didn't mean anything[1]. Gingerly, she rang the bell, fully expecting a complete stranger to answer the door. An annoyed one, at that. When the door opened, she felt both relieved and utterly wretched.

Laxmi's mother stood at the door. Parvathi Swaminathan had been a vivacious woman in her youth, but you would never have guessed it now. The corners of her eyes, the tip of her nose, were pink from crying. Her face looked swollen and her long curly hair, once shiny black and the

1 In Mumbai, people routinely rent out their homes, while keeping their own nameplates firmly nailed to the door. Wanting your own nameplate if you're renting someone else's home is like wanting a man who's deeply attracted to you, just for your well-preserved collection of 14th century history books. You can keep wanting, but it's not going to happen.

envy of other mothers, was now grey and lifeless like the expression on the face under it. Her brow creased when she saw Avantika.

'Yes?' she asked.

And at that very instant, Avantika realized her mistake. She was intruding on this poor woman's sorrow. And why? Out of curiosity. She was about to make up some nonsense about having the wrong address, when suddenly the woman's face cleared.

'Aren't you—? Avantika!' she said, her voice full of wonder.

Too late, Pandit. You idiot.

'Hi Aunty,' she said, hating herself, 'I ... I just heard ... Um ... I'm so ... sorry.'

Pithy, empty words. The woman had just lost her only daughter and here she was, visiting after a decade, more than a decade, saying she was sorry. Stupid, inconsiderate *idiot.*

Laxmi's mother sniffed.

'Come in,' she said, her voice heavy.

The house looked different from the last time she had seen it. The walls, a pale pastel shade of blue, seemed freshly painted. The 80s-style TV unit had disappeared. In its place, a sleek LED TV hung from the wall, facing a white leatherette couch and chairs, successors to the old wooden sofa set with the embroidered cushions. Laxmi's mother gestured to the couch and asked her if she wanted some water.

Avantika shook her head and sat down, but Laxmi's mother went into the kitchen and brought out a glass of water anyway. Hospitality was not something Avantika needed right now, but this instinct to offer water and food to guests seemed to be hardwired into women of that generation. She shuffled on the sofa, as Laxmi's mother sat on a chair opposite her. Silence bloomed. She cleared her throat.

'Um ... how did—,' she began.

'How did you ... get to know?' Laxmi's mother asked at the same time.

Avantika decided to spare her the details.

'Uh... Aisha's brother told me,' she said.

Laxmi's mother nodded.

'She's such a good girl,' she said, 'I don't know what we would have done without her help. She volunteered to go to the hospital, you know. Even when Laxmi's father ...,' she turned to Avantika, a pleading look in her eyes. 'He's not ... he doesn't know how to express what he feels, you understand. When he's sad, disappointed, he just ... he shouts—'

Avantika nodded. She knew this. She'd *seen* this.

'So when Aisha brought the news, he ... you know. All kinds of things he said, as if it was her fault, the poor girl. And all she said was, "Uncle, we can decide whom to blame later, right now we need to go to the hospital".' She sniffed. 'Such a good girl.'

Avantika sipped on her water, to avoid a response. Good girl. Aisha. Yeah.

'Has Uncle gone to ... ', Avantika couldn't bring herself to say the word, '... gone there?'

Laxmi's mother gave her a distraught look.

'He's sleeping inside. He ... he came back and he couldn't speak,' she said. 'Doctors there said it's shock.

When I try to talk to him, he only weeps, that also without making a sound.'

She broke down. Avantika rushed to her side and awkwardly put an arm around her. She didn't know what to say. So she just sat there, rubbing the poor woman's shoulder gently. It seemed to work. A few minutes later, Laxmi's mother took a deep breath and composed herself.

'Sorry—,' she said, her cheeks wet with tears.

'Is there someone I can call?' Avantika asked, 'The neighbours? A relative? You shouldn't be alone, Aunty.'

She shook her head absently.

'My sisters are coming,' she said. 'One from Vashi and one from Kandivali. But it will take time, you know what the traffic is like, no? They can't come by train at their age, how many times I had told Laxmi's father, let's sell this place and shift somewhere that side, but no. Now look, we need our people and there's nobody.'

'I'm sorry.'

Mrs Swaminathan gave a half-smile through the tears and took Avantika's hand in her own hands, soft and veined with age.

'No, no, don't say sorry, it's you girls, you, Aisha, Shweta who are here right now, no? Helping us.'

'I'm not ... Shweta?'

'She works at the hospital where ... they brought Laxmi. She's from your class, you don't know her?'

'Shweta ... Kakkar?' Avantika asked. 'No. Sure. I know her.'

'They found a wallet on the ... Laxmi's wallet, you know. Shweta saw it and she immediately called Aisha. Then Aisha came here to tell us and then Laxmi's father went there. Aisha said he saw her and just froze. She brought him home and then went back to complete the formalities.' Her grip tightened on Avantika's hand and for a moment she looked as if she would break down again. But she took a deep breath instead and a faraway look came into her eyes.

'I used to peel grapes for her, you know,' she said, 'when she was a baby. She couldn't eat the skins, so I used to peel and slice each grape for her. I didn't want her to choke, you know. So much care I took and now—'

This time, she did break down.

Avantika looked around helplessly. Then, struck by a thought, she got up from the couch. 'Aunty, wait, I'll get you some tea,' she said, hurrying off to the kitchen.

It was a cowardly thing to do, but she needed to do something, anything. To help this woman and to escape the deathly silence. The kitchen was modular, done in tones of blue and grey, safe, organized and designed to appeal to upper middle-class sensibilities. Still, it meant Avantika would have to rifle through half a dozen drawers to find the tea things. Just then, her gaze fell on the stainless steel coffee filter[2] next to the gas stove. She heaved a sigh of relief and set about, pouring coffee and milk into a ceramic mug.

After heating the mug in the microwave, she took it into the living room from where, to her horror, Laxmi's mother had disappeared. Avantika had a brief moment of panic. The front door was shut. She hadn't heard it open. Hoping, wishing, praying that she'd find her in one of the bedrooms,

---

2 The stainless steel coffee filter is to the traditional south Indian household what a Tumblr account is to a millennial. You've totes got to have one, bro.

Avantika headed that way. She found Laxmi's mother sitting on the bed in Laxmi's room, a vacant expression on her face.

'Aunty?' Avantika whispered, touching her shoulder gently.

She seemed to snap out of a daze. With an empty smile, she looked at the cup in Avantika's hands, as if not sure what it was. Avantika eased it into her hands, gently urging her to drink as she sat on the bed beside her. A few moments passed. Avantika's gaze fell on the dhurrie on the floor. It had a black and red Aztec pattern on it. She was studying the weave, when Laxmi's mother spoke again.

'It doesn't make sense,' she said, in a bemused voice. 'Why did she run away like that? And that SMS. It doesn't make sense.'

Don't pry, Avantika told herself, don't say anything, don't say—

'What SMS?' she asked.

'Her SMS,' Laxmi's mother murmured, as if speaking to herself. 'The day she left, we got an SMS from her. Same message on both our phones. "Appa will never let me marry who I want to, so I'm going away", it said. Why would she think—?' she trailed off.

'Was she seeing someone Uncle didn't like?' Avantika asked.

Laxmi's mother shook her head absently. 'No. I don't know. When he saw the SMS, he got angry and deleted it. Then he deleted it from my phone also and told me never to bring up the topic again.'

Avantika nodded. Laxmi's father had a legendary temper. Whenever she had visited Laxmi in the past, if her father was home, the two girls would invariably hang out in Laxmi's room as quietly as possible, with the door closed. The thought of this man, whom she was once scared of, being reduced to tears and rendered speechless, upset Avantika in a way she couldn't describe. She glanced at Laxmi's mother. She was sitting with the mug in her hands, the untouched coffee going cold, her eyes devoid of emotion.

'Aunty, do you want me to check where your sisters have reached? If you can give me the numbers, I'll make the calls.'

'No, no, you sit. I'll call them myself.'

And with that, she got off the bed and walked out of the room.

Avantika looked around, trying to find something familiar. This room too had been revamped, since she had last been here. The Madonna poster was gone, as was the ancient wooden almirah where Laxmi used to keep her clothes. In its place was a snazzy wardrobe that covered an entire wall and reached the ceiling. The wooden shelves that once served as Laxmi's own little library had been replaced with floating glass shelves, more in keeping with the modern decor. Only Laxmi's old wooden study desk remained, with the Angelpoise lamp on it.

It was the only reminder of the time she had spent in this room. Now, as she walked to the desk, it all came back to her. Laxmi giggling while drawing a caricature of Mrs Gupta, their geography teacher. Laxmi listening intently as she, Avantika practised the speech she had prepared for the inter-school elocution competition. Laxmi solemnly reading out the poems she had written herself. Gossiping with Laxmi, confiding in her, laughing hysterically over the Mills & Boons they'd found at the local raddiwala[3]. She felt her eyes moisten, as she touched the edge of the desk. The wood was stained with rings left by decades of coasterless coffee mugs. But unlike their school desks, with their endless doodles done in ink and the sharp edge of a geometry compass, Laxmi's desk was pristine. It seemed almost out of place among the steel and laminate of the rest of the furniture in the room.

Avantika wondered why it hadn't been replaced like the rest of the old furniture. The answer came to her in a sudden spark of memory. They had been sitting in Laxmi's room and talking about how the fundamental rights they had been taught about in civics class, did not include a right to privacy. Avantika, whose family had lived in a one-bedroom house at the time, was all for privacy. Laxmi had

---

3 While it is debatable whether Indians invented artificial insemination and nuclear weapons like some political parties claim, it can be said with some confidence that we were recycling before the world turned green. The scrap man or raddiwala would come around with a pair of scales, weigh your old newspapers and magazines and glass bottles and plastic oil cans and pay, I repeat, *pay* you to take them away. At some point, these enterprising folks began to moonlight as old booksellers, which meant you could buy anything from old chemistry textbooks to back issues of *Playboy* from a dingy little shack with heaps of newspapers piled outside. In other words, what goes around, comes around to someone else, and possibly makes them come.

sympathized. Then, her eyes shining, she had asked her if she wanted to see something cool. And without waiting for an answer, she had ...

Avantika stared at the desk for a long moment.

1994

'Wo-ow,' Avantika said, her mouth open, 'This is like something in a Nancy Drew book!'

Laxmi had just fiddled under the desk and a hidden panel—an actual hidden panel!—had slid out from the side! It was quite shallow really, more like a tray than a drawer. Avantika grazed her finger along its sides. She couldn't believe these things existed! It was like finding a baby dragon inside a *chivda* box.

'What do you keep inside it?' she asked.

'Oh, just things I don't want Amma-Appa to find out,' Laxmi said with an impish grin.

Avantika shook her head in wonder.

She had stopped over on the way to their tuition class. She and Laxmi went for maths tuitions to Thyagarajan aunty's place on Mondays, Wednesdays and Fridays. Aunty lived in the building next to Laxmi's so it was convenient to have a quick after-school snack at her place before sinking into the marshlands of mathematics. They had just finished some delicious chilli-cheese toast that Laxmi's mom had made, and their steel plates and glasses stood on the desk, waiting to be taken back to the kitchen.

'Do your parents know about it?' Avantika asked.

'I don't think so,' Laxmi said. 'They've never asked me about it. Appa bought the desk from some old furniture shop, for cheap. I don't think the shopwalla also knew, otherwise he would have told Appa, no?'

Avantika stared at the desk. It looked so ordinary. But a secret panel!

'I wish I had a desk like this,' she said, looking at it longingly. 'I'd hide my maths test paper in it.' She didn't mention the photo of Aamir Khan that she had cut out of her cousin's *Filmfare*. She needed a good hiding place for that too.

Laxmi laughed.

'It's not that bad, Avanti,' she said, 'I'm sure Uncle-Aunty won't scold you very much.'

Avantika made a face. 'We're never going to use half the things they teach us in maths, once we get out of school.'

'We're not going to use poems in real life either, but we still have to study them,' Laxmi said, sitting sideways on the chair, dangling her feet.

'That's okay,' Avantika said.

Laxmi stuck her tongue out at her. 'Ya, ya, because you're good at it it's okay.'

Avantika threw a pillow at her. It missed Laxmi but hit a steel glass on the desk, which fell to the floor with a clang. Avantika froze. Laxmi grinned, 'It's okay, Appa isn't home yet.'

Avantika breathed out, 'I'm more scared of your father than mine.'

'I know. Amma says he's just in a bad mood all the time because he works so hard.'

'When I grow up, I want a job where I can just sit and read all day. You think they have jobs like that?'

'You could be a newsreader! They read *all* the time.'

'Shee, they read such boring and depressing things. These many people died, vegetable prices have gone up. And you have to wear a saree and look serious. Who wants to do all that?'

'Ya, that is there. Then ... a librarian?'

Avantika brightened up. 'Ae, that's a nice one! There will be so many books all around and I just have to say "Ssshh" at people who make noise!'

'Like that Aisha and her group,' Laxmi said with a frown. 'How much they were laughing in library period today!'

'You know, at first I thought they were laughing at me.'

'Don't be silly, Avanti. Why would they laugh at you?'

'I don't know. I swear I thought that Mahira was looking at me and giggling.'

'Mahira giggles at everything. Forget about her.'

Avantika nodded, unconvinced. 'Which book did you take to read?' she asked her, changing the subject.

'*First Term at Mallory Towers*.'

'Is it good?'

Laxmi's face lit up. 'It's very nice! It's about these girls at a boarding school and all the fun they have.'

'Great. I'll borrow it after you're done.'

'It's a whole series by Enid Blyton. Do you like Enid Blyton?'

'I love his books! Have you read the Brer Rabbit ones? They're so funny.'

But Laxmi was laughing. 'Enid Blyton is a woman, silly,' she said amidst giggles.

Avantika felt stupid, so she did what she always did when she felt like that. She drew herself up and said, 'So what? As if *you* know everything.'

Laxmi gave her a good-humoured grin. 'Oh, don't get angry.'

'I'm not angry. Why should I get angry about some stupid book?'

'Hey!' Laxmi wasn't dangling her feet anymore. 'It's not a stupid book. It's better than whatever book you picked!'

'You're wrong!' Avantika said, 'Because mine is a *Famous Five*, not some book about some stupid boarding school.'

Laxmi frowned at her. 'Let's just go for tuitions, we're getting late,' she said quietly.

In silence, they picked up their school bags and left. Avantika was feeling angry, mostly at herself. Why had she behaved like that? She had been irritated since the library episode. She remembered the look on Mahira's face. She'd had the expression of someone who had seen someone else do something ... naughty. And she'd definitely been laughing when Avantika was reading her book. But why? Was it the book? But no, that couldn't be it. You'd have to have a really dirty mind to find something naughty about *Five Visit Billycock Hill.*

Four

Avantika reached under the desk. At first she felt nothing, but a little grappling led her to a smooth wooden knob, roughly the size of a dice. She gave it an experimental twist, then another. And then suddenly, there it was. The hidden panel. It had been empty when Laxmi had shown it to her all those years ago. There was a slim, leather-bound notebook in it now. Avantika stared at it, not sure if she wanted to open it. It could be anything. A doodle-pad. An address book. It could even be blank. But even as she thought this, a part of her knew it was all nonsense. This was a secret panel. It wasn't a place to keep a blank book. It was a place to keep your secrets.

She picked the notebook up. The pages were made from a thick parchment kind of paper. And the leather cover seemed to be cut by hand. The binding, too seemed raw, as if someone had stitched it by hand. It didn't look or feel like anything that could be bought in a shop. She opened it. The first page was a dedication.

LAXMI.
YOU ARE MY ONLY LOVE,
MY ONLY HOPE,
MY ONLY REASON TO LIVE.
AJAY

Avantika raised an eyebrow. Heavy stuff. Whoever Ajay was, he seemed to have it bad for Laxmi. She turned the page. This one had Laxmi's familiar spidery scrawl.

TO AJAY
You walk with grace
On the face
Of my mind
And my glad eyes
Follow although
They know
It's unwise.

She scanned the pages quickly, without really reading them. Each page had a poem, dedicated to Ajay. Yes, she thought, Laxmi was definitely seeing someone. Or had been seeing someone, a man she felt very deeply for. Does he know what's happened? And here, a dangerous thought began to form in her mind. *Did he have something to do with it?* Avantika closed the notebook and was wondering whether to tell Laxmi's mom about it, when the bell rang.

Probably Aunty's sisters, she thought. There was some murmuring and then, a shocked voice said, 'What? Where is she?'

Avantika knew that voice. She had heard it not very long ago, at a press conference she hadn't wanted to attend. Avantika knew she had seconds to spare before Aisha barged into the room and found her standing there, the hidden panel open and a guilty look on her face. She did what any reasonable person would do at a time like this.

She froze for a whole two seconds.

Then, her instincts shot a dirty look at her brain and jumped into action. She snapped the hidden panel shut and was about to punch the air when she realized that notebook was still in her hand. Swearing under her breath, she looked around for someplace to hide it. She could hear footsteps just outside the room. She shoved the notebook in her bag and grabbed an old magazine lying on the desk. Then, with studied nonchalance, she pretended to read the cover.

'What. Are. You. Doing. Here.'

Avantika looked up from the cover and feigned surprise. 'Oh hey, Aisha,' she said.

'Don't.' Aisha said coldly. 'Why are you here?'

'I heard about Laxmi and—'

'And you thought wow, what a scoop. Designer's best friend found dead.'

Avantika flinched as if she had been slapped. 'What the ... who thinks like that? Are you fucking nuts?'

'So why you here then?'

'Because ... God. I don't know, I couldn't believe it, I wanted to ... I was hoping I'd come here and find out that it was some terrible misunderstanding or something.'

'You expect me to believe that?'

'She was my friend too, Aisha.'

'Was.'

'Hey, look—'

'No, you look. She's gone, okay? It's real. And it doesn't involve you.'

'But—'

'Who told you, anyway?'

'Your brother,' replied Avantika. 'I had gone to your place for our interview and—'

'Dhruv? Dhruv told you ... ' she gave a laugh, half disbelieving, half frustrated. 'That was stupid of him. Look, fine, okay? I believe you. I believe you didn't come here looking for a story. But now that you have one, are you going to write it? Because Uncle-Aunty don't deserve more pain in their lives right now.'

Avantika looked at her suspiciously. Genuine consideration for other people's lives and feelings? Who was this person and where had the real Aisha gone?

'I agree,' she said.

'Good, good,' Aisha said, running her hands through her hair nervously. 'So this won't get out then?'

'Not under my by-line,' Avantika said.

'Thank you,' said Aisha.

Avantika nodded. 'Let me know if you need any help with ... you know ... things. The funeral and stuff.'

And now, we wait for a polite 'fuck off', she thought. Mistakenly, as it turned out.

'There won't be a funeral as such. We're taking her to Chandanwadi. Electric crematorium. Eco-friendly. Laxmi would've wanted that.'

Avantika raised her eyebrows. She didn't remember Laxmi as much of a green warrior. People change, she told herself. And remember, you've been out of touch for years. You don't know what she is like now. Was. She cringed inwardly and turned to leave. Halfway to the door, she turned around.

'How did it happen?' she asked Aisha. 'I'm not asking because ... I'm asking for me.'

Aisha's face was blank.

'Accident,' she replied. 'She fell in the sea.'

Avantika nodded absently and left. It was only when she reached her parked scooter that she realized that she was still holding the magazine from Laxmi's room. And that Laxmi's secret notebook was inside her bag.

'Don't you have *any* work?' Uday asked in wonder.

Avantika looked up from her computer screen and minimized the Facebook page open on it. 'I do. I just ... don't want to do it.'

Uday raised an eyebrow.

'It's a *listicle*,' she said, pouring as much scorn as possible into the word. 'Twenty-five ways to get back at your ex. I don't even know *five* and it's not like I haven't thought about it, believe me.'

Uday shrugged. 'Couldn't understand why you were with him anyway.'

'Rishi? Look, we all do stupid things in college, okay? I did ... him.'

'No, that part I get,' Uday said, grinning. 'It's the three years after college that's the mystery.'

It was her turn to shrug. 'I don't know, I guess I thought nobody else would want to date me.'

He gave her a disbelieving look.

'What? I was chubby back then, remember?' she said.

'You were *not* chubby. And even if you had been, you deserved a lot better than him.'

She narrowed her eyes, 'You're being nice to me,' she said in an accusatory tone, 'why?'

'I don't know. Maybe I should see a doctor after work,' he shot back. 'How did that interview go, by the way? Was it as bad as you'd thought?'

Avantika hesitated. Uday was a good friend, but she wasn't sure she wanted to tell him all that had happened. Not yet, anyway.

'No, it was great,' she said. 'Mostly because Aisha wasn't there.'

'Meaning?'

'She wasn't there. She had to be someplace else.'

'But didn't you go all the way till—?'

'Yes.'

'And she didn't send a message cancelling or anything?'

'No.'

'Wow.'

'Yeah.'

'But if the interview didn't happen, where were you all morning?'

She threw her hands up in mock indignation. 'What are you? My mother? I was stuck in traffic.'

He snorted. 'Really? All morning in traffic?'

'This is *Bombay*, you know.'

'Actually it's Mumbai, but okay. At ease, soldier. You can go back to stalking people on social media now.'

She made a face at him as he went back to his seat. Stalking people on social media! Hah! As if she didn't have better—

Suddenly, she went very still. Perhaps it wasn't such a bad idea after all.

Ajay. Terribly prosaic name. Common. You knew at least one Ajay in your lifetime. So did everyone else, including Ajay himself, whoever he may be. Which is why it struck Avantika as strange that there wasn't a single Ajay in Laxmi's friend list. There was no mention of him on her timeline either. Or any now-mandatory lovey-dovey couple selfies for that matter. How can the man you were clearly besotted with, not feature prominently on your Facebook page? Were there no laws anymore?

She glanced at Laxmi's diary lying on her desk, hidden under a magazine. Some of the poems in it had been a bit, well, PG15. She shouldn't have read them, she knew. But she had. She picked it up now, opened a random page and read:

They say I'll be ruined
if I love with my heart
But in matters of affection
The mind plays no part
Now the coin is tossed
Let's begin the game
Heads, for a happy ending
Tails, for just shame.

Who was this man who was going to bring her shame? And did she mean 'just' as in 'only' or 'just' as in justified? That was the problem with having a good vocabulary. Anything could mean anything. She wondered what happened to letting things be. It was as if the starry-eyed cub reporter she had once been had woken up from the sleep she had been drugged into. That chick was nosy. And insane. This couldn't possibly turn out well.

She turned her attention back to Laxmi's profile. So, no Ajay. Maybe he was one of those people who went on a social media detox from time to time. Fine. She just had to find someone who knew about him and his relationship with Laxmi. Like Aisha. Okay, correction, she just had to find someone who knew about him and his relationship with Laxmi, who wouldn't ask her to fuck off when asked to comment on the matter. Easy-peasy.

She scrolled down Laxmi's friend-list. Nearly everyone from the batch of 1999. Definitely all the cool kids, a surprising number of whom seemed to be in touch with Laxmi, judging from her timeline. But then, she had definitely been popular after becoming besties with Aisha. See, Luke, she thought, that's the power of the dark side. As she scrolled down the timeline, one post caught her eye. A chirpy little message from Mahira Hussein née Jariwala saying: 'Hey gurl! just heard! Soooohpy 4 u gaiz! godbless!' followed by eleven different emojis.

After spending a few moments getting over this unprovoked assault on language, she turned the message over in her head. It could've been about anything. Anything. But what if it wasn't? Wasn't it worth a shot? Even if it meant meeting a woman who was robbing some village somewhere of an idiot?

This is a new low, thought Avantika, as she stared at the entrance of Indigo Deli. It wasn't the place that was at fault. She quite liked the Deli's food—she could've written sonnets to their pulled pork burger. And ballads to their homemade mint blueberry ice cream. No, the problem was that she had now been waiting for—she looked at her watch - half an hour. Not for Ryan Gosling, but for *Mahira*, a woman so daft she had mentioned her actual mobile number on her Facebook page. Who *does* that? Okay, granted, it had made it easier to reach her and set up what promised to be a reunion out of a Woody Allen film, but still who *does* that? There was no justice in the world, she decided.

She was about to order something to eat when Mahira sashayed in. The years had been kind to her. Either that or she knew some very expensive surgeons, Avantika thought uncharitably. She was wearing a powder blue shift dress with matching heels and carrying a cobalt blue envelope clutch. Large Jackie O styled sunglasses pushed back dark brown hair with golden highlights. She looked every inch the socialite and heads turned as she made her way to Avantika's table.

'Hi! *Sorry* I'm late!' she squealed and Avantika could hear the exclamation marks.

'Hi,' she replied and forced herself to politely receive the air kisses Mahira gave her.

'I was so surprised when you called! After all these years! It's been so long, na?'

Avantika admitted that it had indeed been a while.

'You know, I had sent you a friend request on FB,' Mahira said, 'but you didn't reply and I was like, why is she giving me so much attitude? Then I figured I had put my *married* name on my FB profile, so I was like maybe that's why Avantika didn't accept my request! Because hello, she didn't know it was *me*!'

Avantika had known exactly who it was, but she decided that Mahira didn't need to know that. 'I'm so glad you understand,' she said instead. 'Are you hungry? Let's order.'

Mahira glanced through the menu and pursed her lips.

'I don't know ... I'm on a greens only diet right now and they don't have a kale smoothie or anything ...'

Avantika nodded sympathetically. As far as she was concerned, diets were like a colon cleanse[1]. Some people had to have them, they helped apparently, but she wouldn't have signed up for one just for kicks.

'Hmm, I'll just have the green tea I guess,' Mahira said.

Avantika beckoned the waiter. 'A green tea and a cappuccino,' she said. As the waiter nodded and left, she turned to Mahira, 'So ... what've you been up to?'

'I have my own business,' Mahira said proudly. 'I do interiors.'

'Wow, nice, where is your—'

'I've just done up my home and my husband's office right now, but he promised that he'd get me more clients soon.'

'That's—'

'He says I have great taste! And he should know, you know. He is really smart.'

---

1 And in many ways, some are.

'Really. What does he do?'

'Oh, he runs his family business. V. R. Screws.'

Avantika was saved from the necessity of responding by the waiter, who came up with their order.

'What about you?' Mahira asked, as the waiter placed a cup of clear green tea before her. 'What does your husband do?'

Not exist, Avantika wanted to reply. Instead, she smiled and added some sugar to her coffee before saying, 'Oh, I'm single.'

Mahira looked apologetic.

'I am *so* sorry,' she said in tones people reserve for funerals.

'Why? It's awesome.'

'But you must feel so lonely, no?'

'Not really.'

'Oh, *good* for you, sweetie!' Mahira said with a sweet smile, as she patted Avantika's hand.

'Anyway,' said Avantika, through clenched teeth. 'Are you in touch with anyone from school?'

Almost immediately, she regretted asking such a broad question. Because judging from the names she rattled off, it seemed Mahira was in touch with *everyone*. Teachers, seniors, juniors and nearly half of their class at the very least. After about ten minutes of listening to what was going on in random strangers' lives, Avantika interrupted her, 'Hey, you know who I ran into the other day? Aisha.'

'Oh! Where?' Mahira asked with a delighted look on her face.

'At a press conference,' Avantika replied, 'She designs bags and I—'

'I know! Aren't they amazing? I already have three!'

'Yes, she had organized this press conference to—'

'Oh my god! I'm dying for her next collection to come out!'

'Ye-ah, we all are,' Avantika said. 'The thing is, I totally forgot to ask her if she's still in touch with Laxmi. You remember La—'

'Hello! Of course, I do! I met her just a few weeks ago! She's into branding now, so I asked her if she could do the brand identity for my business. You know? Logo, visiting card, letterheads, that kind of thing. So anyway, she said she was really busy then, but she said she'd call me soon. At first I was like way to avoid me Laxmi, but then Shweta told me that she and Aisha are doing some joint venture, so I was like okay, that's definitely a big opportunity. Businesswise also and relationship-wise also. You remember that whole thing between her and Aisha's brother, no?'

Avantika frowned. Now that Mahira mentioned it, she did remember hearing bits and pieces of rumours about how Laxmi was dating Dhruv Juneja. But by the time she had heard about it, she and Laxmi were no longer close enough for her to ask about details or receive them, for that matter. Well, it wasn't like she couldn't know them *now*...

'Laxmi went out with Aisha's brother?' she asked, feigning surprise, 'I didn't know—'

Mahira's eyes gleamed. 'Shut up!' she said, excitedly. 'They were dating for like, five years! It started in the tenth standard and we were all so jealous of her! He was such a stud! Soooo good-looking and charming! My god! I was half-mad over him, everyone who met him was half-mad over him! How can you not know this?'

Avantika gave a self-deprecating shrug. 'So ... they're still together?' she asked, continuing her act of least clued-in journalist in the world.

'No, no,' Mahira scoffed, taking a delicate sip of her green tea. 'They broke up after college, I think. Dhruv got married to some society chick afterwards—family friend, you know. But I hear they got divorced last year.' She lowered her voice. 'Apparently she told him she just didn't love him anymore.'

Avantika winced inwardly, but didn't let the look of eager interest slip from her face. 'So you think Laxmi is trying to get back with Dhruv?' she asked. 'But I'd heard she was dating someone called Ajay ... something?'

'Reely?' Mahira asked wide-eyed with excitement, 'Are you sure? I mean, Shweta would've told me if that was the case—'

'Maybe she doesn't know,' Avantika said, taking a sip of water.

'Yeah right,' Mahira laughed. 'Shweta knows *everything* about everyone in our gang.'

She does, does she, thought Avantika with an inward smile.

Mahira was prattling on, oblivious to the dark plotting in Avantika's brain. 'But even if there is some other guy, don't tell me he's better than Dhruv Juneja. I mean, hello? He's rich, he's hot, they have a history. What more do you need?'

Compatibility? Chemistry? A working brain? Avantika pursed her lips, trying not to answer that question.

'You know,' Mahira was saying, 'I think I'll call and meet Laxmi for lunch anyway, you want to join us?'

Sure, Avantika thought, maybe we could ask David Lynch to direct the whole thing. We could call it Lunch by Lynch. Thankfully, the waiter chose this exact moment to hover at her elbow. 'Anything else, ma'am?' he asked.

Mahira shook her head. Avantika, on the other hand, was feeling a bit peckish.

'Can I have the pecan pie from the specials, please?' she asked.

The waiter made a note and left. She turned back to find Mahira glaring at her. She looked outraged.

'How can you do that?' she hissed, 'aren't they like a protected species?'

Avantika blinked.

'What?'

'Hello, aren't they like dying out?'

'Who?'

'Pecans!'

'Pecans?'

'Ya-ha?'

'What?'

'Aren't you journalist types supposed to like, know this stuff? It's this big bird with a huge beak. There was a whole movie with Julia Roberts and everything.'

'That's a pelican,' Avantika said.

'Reely?'

'Yes.'

'You sure?'

'Yes.'

'Oh. Then what's a pecan?'

'A nut.' Like you, she added mentally.

Twenty minutes and a very hurried, humane pecan pie later, Avantika was out of there. At least now she could take an educated guess as to why Mahira had congratulated Laxmi in her post. The history lesson featuring Dhruv was a bonus she didn't know what to do with. And she still didn't have a clue who Ajay was. But thanks to Mahira, she now had the telephone number of someone who might.

Five

'The subscriber you are trying to reach is currently unavailable,' the automated voice told her. Avantika hung up in exasperation. This was the third time she had tried Shweta's number. She drummed her fingers impatiently. She had really hoped to have a chat with Shweta. Possibly more fruitful a chat, than the one he'd had with Mahira. It was obvious that Shweta was more clued in to Laxmi's life. There was a decent chance she might even know the mysterious Ajay.

Of course, whether she'd be willing to tell Avantika anything about him was a different matter. Shweta wasn't like Mahira. She was sharp, difficult to fool and didn't have any particular reason to like Avantika. Getting anything out of her would be difficult. But all that was moot if she was unreachable. How weird would it be to land up at the hospital where she worked unannounced, Avantika wondered. Stop it, she told herself, you're veering into lunatic territory here. What she needed was another point of view. A neutral person, whom she could run this idea by, to beta-test its madness quotient, so to speak. It was time to talk to Uday.

Uday's desk was a few feet away from Nathan's cabin. Avantika scanned the area, wondering how to get there without being noticed by Nathan. Then she froze. A man was coming out of Nathan's cabin. A very *familiar* man. He noticed her staring and gave her a friendly smile.

'Hi there,' Dhruv Juneja said.

Avantika opened her mouth to speak, then shut it. There were any number of reasons why he could be visiting the *Mumbai Daily* office. Just because none of them were popping into her head right this minute did not mean they didn't exist. Also, she was probably feeling a little lightheaded because of dehydration or something. Definitely nothing to do with this man. Definitely.

'Hi,' she said. 'Do you umm ... come here often?'

How is it, she wondered, that something that sounds casual and witty in my head, sounds utterly idiotic when I actually say it?

Dhruv grinned anyway. Goddamned dimples.

'Only on days that end with Y,' he said. 'No, I'm actually here because I'm doing a project for you guys. A weekly photo series on heritage architecture in Mumbai.'

'Cool,' said Avantika. 'So I'll ... we'll be seeing a lot more of you then.'

'I *could* just email stuff across,' he said, 'but if someone *wants* me here, I suppose I could drop by.'

Whoa. Wait. Hold on a second. Avantika blinked.

'Great,' she managed to say before the pause got too long. 'Good to know.'

'You got me into trouble that day, you know.'

'Sorry?'

'With my sister,' he explained. 'Apparently, I wasn't supposed to tell you about Laxmi.'

'Oh,' she said, 'sorry about that. Do you always do what you're supposed to?'

He gave her an embarrassed smile. 'It's a terrible habit, but I'm trying to quit.'

'Well, you know what they say. Admitting you have a problem is the first step.'

He laughed.

'How do I not remember you?' he asked.

'Well, I came around just the one time, we didn't really *meet* meet.'

'When was this?'

Avantika cringed inwardly. This was one trip down memory lane that she wasn't keen on. 'I don't remember,' she lied.

'Now why don't I believe that?' he asked.

'Wow, you're all about the questions, aren't you?' she muttered.

'Sorry, it's just ... wait, were you the one who had come over to stay that summer?'

'Definitely not.'

'Were you at the seventh standard pyjama party?'

'No.'

'The ninth standard pyjama party?'

'No.'

'Were you on the basketball team? Those girls used to come over all the time.'

Avantika sighed. The man probably meant well, but he was missing a crucial point.

'Look, in case you hadn't noticed, your sister and I aren't exactly ... pals.'

'Ah. Yes. Right. Then when—'

'Hi, I'm Shibani,' said a voice behind her. The girl attached to it was flashing Dhruv a delighted grin.

'Er ... Dhruv Juneja,' he said.

'Oh, I knowwww,' she breathed, shaking his hand warmly, 'I'm a huge fan!'

Dhruv smiled uncertainly. 'Thanks—'

'Nathan just told me about your photo-feature! I'm soooo excited! I'm the arts and culture editor,' she said pointing to herself. 'Do you want to discuss some ideas later in the evening? I know this great place? Awesome music and really cool drinks, you know? Anyway, I just thought I'd introduce myself and ask if you need any help? Because you can totally call me if you need anything, you know?'

Avantika stared at her open-mouthed. How is this woman not teaching a course somewhere, she wondered. Dhruv had a hunted expression.

'Er, sure,' he said, 'But I'm a little busy tonight so—'

'Great, tomorrow night, then,' she said, walking away. 'You can pick me up from here at eight? Awesome.'

They watched her retreating back, which even Avantika had to admit, was an attractive sight, what with the pencil skirt and the heels. Her own sensible flats and skinny jeans were no contest.

'So,' she said lightly. 'That's your weekend sorted.'

'Yeah, right,' Dhruv said.

'No, really,' she said, coming over all serious. 'Shibani has you in her sights now. There is no escape. You better prepare yourself for extreme origami dubstep or something.'

'Extreme what?' he asked, laughing.

'You'll see,' she said in an ominous tone, before walking away towards Uday's desk.

'Who was that?' Uday asked, as she leaned against his desk.

'Dhruv Juneja. Aisha's brother. He's a photographer. Nathan's got him doing some heritage photo feature for us.'

'Seems to like *you*,' Uday muttered.

She gave him a sideways look. 'What makes you say that?'

'Body language,' he said, not taking his eyes off his screen.

'Aren't you supposed to be working on a story? What happened to focusing on the job at hand?'

'It's called multitasking, babe,' he said with a smirk.

She decided to ignore the 'babe'.

'I have a question for you,' she said instead.

'Shoot.'

'If I wanted to get information from someone who I think knows something, hypothetically you understand, and for some reason I can't get in touch with them over the phone, is it totally unacceptable to go over to their workplace unannounced and ask them questions?'

Uday turned away from his computer and gave her a long look. 'What the fuck have you been up to?' he asked.

'Nothing,' she said, trying to look innocent. 'This is just a hypothetical what-if scenario.'

He nodded.

'Sure, sure,' he said. 'Tell me, does it say I'm a moron on my face or is this a conclusion you have arrived at after running some tests on me?'

She made a face. This was not going well. 'You're overreacting,' she told him, 'I just wanted to know—'

'And I just want to know what you have been doing, because it sounds like you have been doing *something* and not a very good something at that.'

She backed away from his desk. 'Forget it,' she said, 'I'll figure it out.'

'Oh no, you won't,' said Uday, getting up. 'Not without telling me what the hell is going on because—' He didn't get a chance to finish, because at that moment the door to Nathan's cabin flew open and Nathan stormed out, his face dark and his voice loud.

'Pandit! My office! Now!'

Uday looked at Avantika.

'What did you do?,' he asked, the argument forgotten.

'Probably something terrible,' said Avantika sourly, 'like breathing.'

1996

Dhug. Dhug. Dhug.

The ball bounced against the steel grey concrete of the basketball court, as girls ran back and forth trying to score a shot. Avantika sat on the stands that had been put up on one side of the court, watching the match with the rest of the girls. It was quite a crowd—a mix of her own classmates from 8A and students from 9B, whom they were playing against today. There were even students from other standards. But then, this was the intra-school semi-final.

Avantika watched as Aisha feinted to the right and escaped from the player designated to shadow her, dribbling the ball furiously as she made her way to the basket at the other end of the court. She was the captain of their team and Avantika had to admit, rightly so. The same growth spurt that had left Avantika howling with achy legs had turned Aisha into a slim, tall girl, who could net a ball with one easy jump. She made a good basketball player. And if Laxmi was to be believed, a good captain as well.

Laxmi! She was on the team as well and that was the only reason Avantika had come to watch the match. Sports was not her thing. Okay, correction, sports was not her thing *anymore*. Especially after she'd tried for and hadn't been picked for the basketball team. Laxmi had, and she was having a blast, from the looks of it. There she was now, jumping up, arms outstretched, asking for the ball, dodging, weaving, trying to shake off the girl who was blocking her. Further down the court, Aisha's opponent had caught up to her. Aisha ignored her and raised the ball high over her head. No way, Avantika thought, she was standing almost at the free throw line, there was no way she could score a point. Aisha leapt, throwing the ball with all the might. It passed neatly through the basket and landed with a satisfying thud on the court. The crowd erupted in cheers and applause.

Avantika clapped grudgingly as Aisha and Laxmi exchanged a high-five on the court. They were becoming friends, Avantika could see. She had hoped it would be a passing thing. But then, the other day, a chit had dropped out of Laxmi's notebook and she'd realized that it was anything but that. It was a FLAMES calculation. She'd seen other girls do those. First you wrote down a boy's name and your name, then you cancelled out all the common letters. Then you wrote FLAMES underneath, counted the remaining letters and cancelled every corresponding letter on the word 'FLAMES,' till you were left with just one. If it was F, it meant you'd be friends forever. If it was L, it meant you'd fall in love and so on. She didn't know any boys interesting enough to warrant a FLAMES calculation from her side. She wanted to do one with Mr Darcy from *Pride and Prejudice*, but Fitzwilliam was such a stupid name. Clearly, Laxmi didn't have many options either because the chit had her and Aisha's name on it. And it had thrown up M for marriage! Har, har, har, like that was going to happen! She had asked Laxmi about it, meaning to tease her, but the girl had just shrugged.

'We were just bored,' she'd said. 'Anyway, who says you can't do FLAMES between girls? M is the only problem. And that doesn't have to mean 'marriage'. It can mean ... it can mean 'mates', you know? Like British people say.'

'Okay,' Avantika had said. 'So ... you and Aisha are mates or what?' The only reason she hadn't used air quotes was because they hadn't been invented yet.

'She's fun,' Laxmi had said, looking away, 'and she's not as bad as you think.'

'But ... but, why do you need to hang out with her so much?' Avantika had asked, trying to keep the jealousy out of her voice.

Laxmi had looked at her as if she had gone mad. And then, worst of all, she had laughed.

'Avantika, don't be silly,' she'd said. 'I hang out with you because I like hanging out with you, no? I hang out with her because ... I like hanging out with her also. With you I can talk about books and drama and with her I can talk about basketball and music and things.'

Music. Pfff. Aisha and her fancy MTV music, which she, Avantika, wasn't allowed to listen to yet. Aai said she should focus on her studies and was there really time to watch MTV when you had to go to tuition class right now? And Baba, he had asked what was wrong with our Indian music, why do you need to listen to this Madonna-Bidona when we had Kishori Amonkar? Parents, she thought bitterly, what did they know? How could she possibly explain that listening to English pop music was an important rung on the social ladder that she would now not be climbing at all, thank you very much? How could she explain to them what 'cool' is? They thought it was a fridge setting.

Another cheer from the crowd brought her reeling back to the present. A girl from the other team had scored a basket. Laxmi looked crestfallen. It seemed she hadn't blocked the girl properly. Aisha placed a sympathetic hand on her shoulder and said a few words to buck her up. It seemed to work, because Laxmi nodded briskly and bounded away on the court.

'Buck up, Laxmeeee!' Avantika yelled over the crowd and clapped. Could her friend hear her? Would it make a difference?

The score was 1–1. The referee, their physical education teacher and coach, Miss Rastogi, blew her whistle in two short blasts indicating a break in the game. She was the only teacher allowed to not wear a sari to school. During PE class she usually turned up in a salwar kameez, dupatta tied firmly to the side. But on match days and interschool sporting events she switched to the smart grey track pants and the modest white t shirt she wore today.

The players huddled in two opposite corners of the court. Ignoring the ouches of girls on whose toes she was inadvertently stepping, Avantika made her way to the corner where the 8A team was sitting. She would almost certainly lose her seat and would have to watch the rest of the match standing up, but that was okay. She needed to talk to Laxmi.

Laxmi was sitting on a low bench, drinking from a bottle of water. Sweat streamed off her in little rivulets and wisps of her long hair had come undone from the tight plait she had tied it into. She was breathing a little heavily. Behind her was the rope, separating the audience from the player area. Avantika reached over the rope and tapped her on the shoulder.

'Laxmi,' she called.

'Oh hi,' Laxmi said. She looked surprised, but happy to see her.

'I just came to tell you that you know, don't let that ... affect you. You're playing really well.'

'It was a stupid mistake, but thanks,' Laxmi beamed.

'And um ... break a leg. No actually, that's what you say before plays, it's probably not the best thing to say now. Um. Good luck, then—'

Aisha, who had been watching their exchange from a distance, came over now. 'Come na, I just want to talk to the team a bit,' she said to Laxmi. She didn't even glance at Avantika.

Laxmi nodded. Then with a quick smile at Avantika, she got up and followed Aisha to the court. Avantika watched them leave, with a sinking sensation in her chest. She was losing Laxmi. She could tell. As she walked back to her seat, leaving another trail of accidentally crushed toes in her wake, she wondered if there was anything she could do to stop it. She, with her books and her loud mouth and her springy hair and her puberty-given sprinkling of acne. Versus Aisha, who was beautiful, rich, talented and charismatic. She already had fans in school. Fans! Like a Bollywood actress.

Not that she was the only one. Academic stars, sports stars, stars of the stage and of inter-school events—at St Agatha, those who shone bright, inevitably attracted eager, adoring followers. Most of them were harmless enough, wide-eyed little moths drawn to the flame of talent. They'd huddle in adoring groups, giggling in the corridors when they passed the usually older girl they worshipped. Or they'd stand at a distance, watching her exploits on say, the basketball court, clapping furiously when she scored and glaring at anyone who dared to boo her.

But sometimes, and these weren't as few as everybody liked to pretend, the admiration would turn into something darker.

Avantika had heard whispers last year, about a girl from the seventh standard who had started writing letters to her ninth standard idol—a girl who'd won several singing competitions—using her own blood for ink. Avantika privately felt that this was a waste of perfectly good haemoglobin. And apparently, the girl had to be taken away for counselling and had missed more than a month of school. Her letters, the whispers claimed, had expressed her undying love and devotion to the other girl. It all seemed a bit ... much, to her.

She reached her seat, and observed without surprise that someone else was sitting there now. The girls sitting behind began yelling at her to stand at the side and not block their view. Shoulders slumped, she shuffled to the end of the row, where the seats ended. The view wasn't that good from here—you could only see what was happening if any players considerately decided to leave the baskets alone and came to stand here solely for your benefit. The place was already packed with girls who hadn't managed to get seats and they were not happy to make room for a newcomer. They pushed and shoved, till she found herself at the very edge of the first row, right in the corner, almost touching the court itself. If any of the teachers noticed, she'd be shooed away for sure. But there was no place anywhere. She decided to just stand there till someone asked her to move.

Just in time, as it turned out, because at that very instant Miss Rastogi blew her whistle again, signalling the end of the break. The second half of the game began and a few minutes later, the 8A team scored another basket. Amidst cheers of 'North-south-east-west-eight-A-are-the-best', Avantika saw the older team shoot murderous glances at her class team. And as the game progressed, it seemed to get rougher. There was more shoving, girls seemed to be tripping and falling all over the place. From the way her whistle kept blowing, Miss Rastogi seemed to be spotting more fouls on the court than at a chicken farm.

Avantika watched with rising excitement as a girl from the opposing team snatched the ball from Laxmi mid-dribble and raced to the other end of the court to shoot. Both teams sped behind her. The scoreboard was tied. It was going to be a close thing. Avantika saw Laxmi trying to defend the basket, leaping in front of her opponent, arms flailing, to keep her from scoring. The girl spun around to dodge her, elbows sticking out, perhaps just a bit more than strictly necessary. There was a dull thud and a muffled groan. The girl scored. The 9B crowd roared. '9B!' clap-clap-clap '9B!' clap-clap-clap.

But something was wrong. Aisha had ignored the ball, the players, the game and was rushing toward Laxmi. To Avantika's horror, she realized her friend was doubled up, face covered, eyes screwed shut. Laxmi was hurt! Without thinking, she turned around and began pushing her way through the throng of girls, trying to reach the other end of the stands, where Aisha seemed to be heading with Laxmi.

By the time Avantika reached, they were surrounded by the rest of the team. She pushed her way through the other players to find Miss Rastogi holding Laxmi's hands.

'Let me see, let me see,' the teacher was saying, as she gently pried the girl's hands away from her face.

Avantika felt a pit open in her stomach. Laxmi's nose was bleeding, tiny red streams flowing down her lip, staining her teeth. A couple of drops had fallen on the pristine white t-shirt, which along with the dark pink divided skirt, was their sports uniform. It wasn't the sight of the blood that was making Avantika's heart pound. She'd started her periods last year and a year of *that* was enough to cure you of any squeamishness at the sight of blood. No, what was making her wince on Laxmi's behalf was the way her friend's nose seemed to have *twisted* a little to the left. The girl was crying with pain, clutching tightly to Aisha's hand, as the other girl tried to calm her with soothing words.

Miss Rastogi peered at the bloody mess that was Laxmi's face and frowned. 'You need to go to the sick room. This needs a doctor.'

'I'll take her, Miss,' Avantika offered, at the same time Aisha did.

'You're in the middle of a game, Aisha,' Miss Rastogi pointed out reproachfully.

Avantika took a step towards Laxmi, but Aisha glared at her, jaw set. 'Let's cancel it and have a rematch, a *fair* one,' she said, shooting a poisonous look at the captain of the other team, who had walked up to see the damage. The girl opened her mouth to protest, but Miss Rastogi beat her to it.

'Don't be ridiculous,' she said with a frown. 'It's the semi-finals and there's a minute left on the clock. Get back on the court.'

But Aisha stood her ground. She was staring at Laxmi's face, which was contorted with pain, and for a moment it seemed as if she couldn't see anything else. 'Then we'll forfeit.'

Avantika was taken aback. Aisha was letting the other team win? Just like that? How would she ever explain that to the team? To the class? They were *this* close to making it to the finals! What was wrong with her?

The others seemed to be just as shocked, because they all begin to protest. Even Laxmi, clearly in agony, groaned, 'I can wait ... ow ... till the game is done.'

It was Avantika's turn to glare.

'You don't need to!' she snapped. 'I'll take you there right away! Didn't you hear what Miss said? You need a doctor, Laxmi!'

Laxmi looked from her to Aisha, then back to her and said with a brave grimace, 'It's okay. Aisha can take me after the game.'

And suddenly on that court crowded with hundreds of people, Avantika felt very, very alone.

Six

Tick tock. Tick tock. The clock ticked away, sounding unexpectedly eerie in the small silent cabin. Nathan hadn't said a word yet. He was just looking at Avantika. No, not looking. He was sitting in his chair, glaring quietly at her, making the suspense mount, making the silence unbearable till—

'You called?' Avantika asked.

'I had a very interesting conversation today. I'll tell you why it was interesting. It was interesting because for the first time in my entire career, I was on a call with a PR rep and I had to just shut up and listen.'

'Oh ... that's—'

'I'm still talking. Not only did I have to listen, I had to apologize at the end of that call. Apologise for something *you* did.'

'What did I—?'

'No, no, no,' Nathan said, playing with the old-fashioned glass paperweight on his desk, 'I talk. You listen. I'm done listening, remember? What the fuck did you think you were doing stalking Aisha Juneja?'

Avantika opened her mouth to laugh. But Nathan looked dead serious.

'I didn't ... what?'

'So you didn't follow her to her friend's house, her recently *deceased* friend's house, and harass that girl's mother for information?'

Avantika felt like the wind had been knocked out of her. 'That's not what ... I didn't ... that's ridiculous, Nathan!'

'I agree. It is ridiculous that someone at *my* newspaper is pulling stunts like this! Do you think this is India bloody TV? It is not!' He leaned forward and for the first time since she'd taken the job, Avantika felt genuinely scared. His voice was a menacing whisper. 'I have put up with a lot of crap to keep this paper running but I will not put up with *this*!'

He sat back and took a deep breath.

'You will apologize. In writing. And you will keep away from Ms Juneja ... which, if you are to be believed, was what you wanted in the first place!'

Avantika grit her teeth. 'I won't say sorry,' she said quietly.

'Oh yes, you will,' Nathan said, holding up a warning finger. 'I've fired people who mean a lot more than you to this paper, for a lot less. My patience with you is running out, Pandit. You turn up your nose at features, you're too chicken to do some actual reporting and you don't seem to have a stop button for your mouth. And guess what? Your designer friend knows some pretty important people. So you're saying sorry or you're out of a job.'

He turned back to yesterday's edition of the *Mumbai Daily* that was lying on his desk. The conversation was clearly over, as far as he was concerned. To hell with *that*, Avantika thought.

'First of all, and I've been saying this since day one, Aisha is not my *friend*' she said, almost slurring over the words in anger, "But you know who was? Laxmi! The girl who died! I didn't go over there to harass anyone, I went there because that's what you do if a friend dies! Secondly, I don't care who Aisha knows and I don't care what they can do. But most of all, Nathan, I can't believe *you* are lecturing *me* about being chicken! We're doing *listicles*, Nathan! Twenty-five ways to wear a messy braid! Thirty ways to make a great first impression! Forty-five ways to use lemongrass in the kitchen! Lemongrass, Nathan, *lemongrass*! Don't fucking tell me about being chicken, when we're going to carry its fucking health benefits the day we're a column short of beauty tips!'

She could feel the pinpricks of angry tears in her eyes. She blinked them back. Nathan had been looking at her without any expression since she had begun her rant.

'Sit down.' His voice was quiet and just as blank as his face.

She breathed out, letting the anger subside just a fraction. Then she sat down.

'Do you know why I hired you?', he asked.

'Because there weren't any typos—'

'Sure, because that's the most important qualification I'd look for in a reporter, right?'

Avantika held up both hands in a 'who knows' gesture. He shook his head.

'I hired you because I know how you ended up at *Belle*.'

Avantika held her breath.

'What do you mean?'

'I know what happened at the *Herald*, Pandit,' he said, leaning back in his chair. 'It wasn't the first time it's happened in our industry and it certainly won't be the last. Quitting your job over it was very ... *idealistic*.'

He may as well have said 'idiotic'. He certainly used the same tone.

'Yes, well,' she said. 'Silly me. I thought MPs being bribed to pass civil work contracts was something people deserved to know about. I didn't think the story would get clamped, by the editor, of all people.'

'Why not?' Nathan asked, eyebrows raised. 'Editors are people too. If you cut us, do we not bleed? If you threaten our families, do we not shit bricks?'

Avantika shrugged.

'Although, in this case,' Nathan said, looking at the ceiling, 'it was Shiv Dharmadhikhari, the owner of the *Herald*, who got threatened. Still, tomaytoes, tomahtoes.'

'I don't care,' Avantika said. 'If I had to do it all over again, I'm not sure I'd act any differently.'

Nathan raised his eyebrows in surprise. 'Really? And here I thought you were the sensible type.'

'Sensible, yes. *Cynical*, no.'

Nathan laughed a bitter, half-hearted laugh. 'Cynics are born from the ashes of idealists, Pandit. Nobody gets into journalism thinking "I want to write pointless drivel nobody cares about". And then you grow up and find out that's *all* anyone cares about.'

He took off his spectacles and blew on them, his breath fogging up the lens.

'You were a reporter before you joined *Belle*. I hired you to see if you were still a reporter. But from what I've seen so far, you're stuck in limbo. Too disillusioned to do real news, not disillusioned enough to like features.'

He held up a hand when she opened her mouth to protest.

'Incidentally, those listicles you're whining about have a readership. A young readership. Do you know what happens when newspapers don't have a young readership anymore? They shut down, Pandit. Ask your Neetu Malini from *Belle*. I'm not exaggerating. The Buzzfeeds and Scoopwhoops of the world are hammering nails in our collective coffin. We need every pair of eyes we can get and if it means putting listicles in the damned paper, hell I'll write one myself!'

He got up and walked to the window, standing with his back to her. On the wall next to him, trapped agelessly in a black-and-white photograph, a younger Nathan laughed at someone's joke.

'Write the apology,' he said, looking out of the window. 'It's not worth fighting for.'

She turned and walked out of his cabin. He was right. And that wasn't even the most depressing thing about that conversation.

Uday was loitering outside the cabin, looking worried. 'What happened, everything okay?'

'Pretty much,' Avantika said not stopping. 'Listen, how do you feel about alcohol?'

Uday's forehead creased in confusion, as he fell in step with her. 'I'm pro it. Where are you going?'

'Someplace that serves alcohol.'

Uday glanced at his watch. It was just after six in the evening. 'Isn't it a little early for that?' he asked.

'Nope,' she said, as she reached her desk. Packing her things into her bag haphazardly she said, 'I'll be just in time for happy hour.'

She closed the bag shut and swung it onto her shoulder. Then, as an afterthought, she grabbed a clean sheet of A4 paper from her desk and began writing as Uday peered over her shoulder.

'*Dear Ms. Juneja,*' he read, '*I apologize for stalking you and invading the privacy of your friends and family. It was an unconscionable act on my part and I am truly sorry for the pain and inconvenience I have caused. I hope you find it in your heart to forgive me. Sincerely, Avantika Pandit.*'

He stared at Avantika, speechless. 'Wait—' he managed, but she ignored him.

Folding the paper neatly, she looked around and spotted Wayne, who happened to be around.

'Hey Wayne,' she said waving him over. 'Can you do me a huge favour?'

The boy looked at her suspiciously. This was a degree of politeness he clearly didn't expect from her. 'Er ... sure,' he said.

She handed him the piece of paper and smiled sweetly at him. 'Can you just hand this over to Nathan Uncle, please? Thanks a ton, I owe you one.'

Then, without missing a beat, she took her bag and set off towards the elevator. Uday, who had snapped out of his shock by now, ran ahead and blocked her path.

'Look, just stop for a second, okay? This isn't some bloody episode of *Newsroom*. Can you just stand still for a minute and tell me what the hell is going on?'

Avantika stopped. She took a deep breath and looked at him. 'No,' she said and walked past him into the elevator, 'but if you come along, you can hear all about it.' She held the elevator door open for him.

Uday stared at her for a second. He had a story to file, a couple of sources to talk to and some facts to cross-check before he was done for the day. On the other hand, what kind of an investigative reporter would he be, if he turned down a story like this?

He grinned.

Seven

'Long. Island. Eyes. Thingy. Drink. Tea? Tea! That's it! That's what I call value for money.'

They were sitting at the bar in Khar Social. Around them, young people of all shapes and sizes lounged on mismatched chairs, paying scant attention to the exposed bricks and chunky pipes—hallmarks of the industrial chic school of interior design. The air was filled with pop music, laughter and earnest voices trying to be witty for the benefit of the opposite sex.

Uday took a swig of his beer and grinned. 'Then how come you're not drinking one?'

Avantika held on to her mojito protectively. 'Because it tastes like crap, duh.'

Avantika had finished telling him about Aisha's incredible accusation somewhere around her second drink. It had been a Cosmopolitan. Or maybe a Moscow Mule. It was hard to say. It had been a while ago.

'Like Jägerbombs,' she continued. 'What is up with those? How can people put something that vile in their mouths? Can you not get drunk on something that tastes good?'

Uday shook his head and smiled. The place was slowly filling up and already he'd gotten a once-over from a rather cute woman in a fetching floral dress. He was considering sending a drink over to her when another woman looked in his direction, her eyes flashing with recognition. This one was wearing a loose tank top and ripped jeans, a scarf thrown idly around her neck. Long, wavy hair and horn-rimmed librarian glasses completed the look. She was pretty in a hipster kind of way, pretty enough for a guy to remember having a conversation with. Uday was sure he hadn't met her before and so had no clue why she was walking towards him so purposefully. He straightened up and squared his shoulders. Maybe he did know her and was having the worst-timed case of amnesia possible. These things happened. Not to him, but they happened. He was about to smile at her when she looked right past him and said, 'Avanti? Oh my god, it's been so long!' She threw her hands around Avantika in a bear hug.

'Vibs!' exclaimed Avantika, returning the hug with a smile more good-natured than any Uday had ever seen her give another human being. 'How are ya?'

'I'm fine, girl,' said Vibs, giving Uday a polite smile. 'What have you been up to?'

'Psssh, work,' replied Avantika. 'Also, drinking. You want some?' she asked, holding out her glass.

The other girl laughed good-naturedly. Uday cleared his throat, hoping Avantika would take the hint and introduce him. They both ignored him.

'Nope, I got my own,' Vibs said, pointing to a girl further down the bar collecting two drinks with umbrellas from the bartender. Then she dropped her voice a bit and asked with genuine concern, 'How've you been holding up?'

Avantika squinted at her. 'I don't know, Vibs,' she said with a shrug, 'life is just screwing around with me these days. But hey, at least I can afford vodka, right?'

The girl nodded in a way that made Uday feel like he was missing a significant amount of subtext.

'You hang in there, girl,' said Vibs rubbing Avantika's arm, 'don't even think about that bastard. I can't believe he'd do that to you.'

'I know!' Avantika said. A second later, she frowned and asked, 'Wait, what?'

'If I were you, I'd go over and punch him the face, that asshole.'

'What are you talking about?'

'Rishi and Natasha,' the girl said, rolling her eyes. Catching the blank look on Avantika's face, she covered her mouth with her hand in horror. 'Oh God! You haven't heard!'

Avantika shook her head but that only made the world swim before her eyes, so she stopped. 'What now?' she asked wearily.

'Avanti, they're getting married next month. I'm so sorry. I thought you knew.'

Avantika gave her a long look. Then she lifted her glass and took a slow sip. Putting the glass down deliberately, she said, 'Good for them.'

Vibs waited for more, but Avantika just looked at her politely. About fifteen seconds of awkward silence later, Uday cleared his throat again.

'Hi, I'm Uday,' he said brightly, 'have we met before?'

It was an hour later. The place had a lot in common with Avantika—both were buzzing. And becoming increasingly noisy.

'I mean ... why, right?' Avantika was saying. 'Why do people feel obl... oblig... like they need to tell me what is happenin' in his life? I don' care. I'm *happy* not knowin'. Don' they ... gethaa?'

Uday shook his head. 'No, they don't. People are dumbasses.'

'Yes! They! Are!' Avantika said, pointing a finger at him emphatically. 'Stupid Vibha. I'm naw even in touch with her! And now I know why!'

She gulped her drink and made a face. It was an appletini. 'Should've stuck to mojitos,' she mumbled.

'Yeah, that's not the problem,' Uday said, shaking his head.

'Whaa?'

'Nothing, never mind.'

'No, no,' she said, squinting at him. 'What did you mean?'

'Look ... it's ... nothing,' he said.

She punched him in the arm and he looked at her, eyebrows raised.

'Really? I go to the gym.'

'Just tell me!'

Kicking himself mentally, he took a swig of beer.

'Alright, here it is. I think you're running away from how pissed off you are at Rishi. You say you don't care what he's doing, but you're sitting here priming yourself for liver poisoning because you just found out he's getting married. You haven't gone out with anyone since you guys broke up. I'm not saying, you know, get on Tinder or anything, but not one date in two years? Come on—'

'Hey, that's because—'

'All I'm saying is, if you're pissed off at him, stop acting like you've moved on. Stop saying you don't care, stop—'

'I *have* moved on, I *do* not care—'

'I saw your face when that chick told you the news! Who're you kidding? You're still hung up over that piece of shit and—,' he broke off with an exasperated sigh. 'Look, it's your life, but throw it away for something better than that moron.'

Avantika glared at him, then her shoulders sagged. 'It's not like that,' she said quietly. The warm glow of alcoholic joy had drained away from her face. Her gaze hardened. 'Rishi and I ... we went out of seven years, off and on,' she said, staring straight ahead of her. 'We'd break off, then get back together, then break off. Over and over again. But you already know that.'

Uday nodded, his face grim.

She closed her eyes for a moment. 'In those seven years, Uday, my head was full of him. Do you understand? I hated him and loved him and just ... fucking hated his guts, because he was such a toxic prick, but I felt those things for him, you know? Even after he cheated on me with Natasha ... I felt angry with her, I felt pissed off with him. And I felt disgusted with myself for taking so long to work out that they were fucking around behind my back. That whole relationship made me hate myself, okay? And all that crap, those ... those are feelings. You can't get rid of seven years of feelings in two years, even if those feelings are mostly ... homicidal.'

She opened her eyes and took a deep breath. Her fingers tightened around the cold sides of her glass. 'At first, I blamed myself. I mean, why would a guy cheat on a girl, if she was great, right? I thought I must've been too demanding, too sarcastic, too I don't know ... maybe not hot enough. But then I thought, okay, that explains why *he* did it. But why did my best friend have to sleep with my fiancé? What kind of asshole does that?' She ran her fingers through her hair and clenched at her scalp.

'The kind that doesn't believe in bros before hoes,' said Uday, patting her back.

'Sisters before misters,' Avantika corrected him. 'That's the one for women. Except in my specific case, it seems the rule is "misters before Avantika" or possibly, "everything before Avantika".'

Uday shrugged and sipped his beer. 'No, wallow, wallow. That's what self-pity is for.'

'I'm serious! This is an actual problem! I'm not anyone's priority friend.'

Uday's brow furrowed. 'Is that a credit card company thing?'

She grinned in spite of herself. 'No, you ass, I meant I don't have any friends for whom I'm the number one priority. You know. Someone they'd drop everything for.'

'Thanks. For your information, there are about half a dozen things I could be doing right now.'

She rolled her eyes. 'I meant *women* friends—'

He shook his head and made a face. 'There's always something with you, isn't it? Here I am, a devastatingly handsome, intelligent, charming, single man—'

'Modest, you forgot modest.'

'... modest man, thank you, who is ignoring all the hot women in this place to be your agony aunt, but no, I must have a uterus too!'

She laughed and took a sip of her drink. He grinned back then looked at the message that had just popped up on his phone.

'Yes, yes, all right, point taken,' she said. 'I mean the world to you and there is nothing more important than me right now.'

Uday looked up from his phone. 'Yeah, I gotta go,' he said.

'What!' she said, throwing her hands up.

'Sorry, you know that Sion murder case? My source just found someone who can talk to me about it. But he needs to meet right now.'

Avantika narrowed her eyes at him in mock menace. 'What the hell happened to chivalry?'

'Don't tell me you forgot? I thought I saw you at the funeral.'

She pointed a threatening finger at him. 'You better make this up to me,' she growled.

'Sure,' he said, waving his credit card at the barman, 'I'll get this.'

She smiled a syrupy little smile, 'Awww!'

'You'll be okay going home on your own?' he asked, ignoring it.

'Sure. Also, awwwwwwww.'

'Yeah, yeah,' said Uday, looking thoroughly disgusted. He gave her a quick one-armed hug before making his way out of the crowd.

She watched him leave and let out a breath. She didn't plan on hanging around much longer. Her glass was almost empty. Perhaps her bloodstream could handle one last drink. She turned to the barman.

'Can I just have a beer, please?'

As he slid her the bottle, she held out her debit card. But he waved it away.

'Oh, that's been paid for,' he told her.

'What? By whom?' she asked.

The barman jerked his head in the direction of the man standing next to her.

'So,' said Dhruv Juneja with a grin, 'you come here often?'

Eight

There are many horrifying ways to wake up. You could wake up in a bathtub filled with ice and suspiciously red water, holding a note that explains the regrettable absence of your kidneys. Or wake up to the cries of your colicky newborn ... and never be able to go back to sleep till that baby turns eighteen and leaves for college. Or, if you're the lead in a Madhur Bhandarkar film, there's the horror of waking up next to the African American gentleman you met in the club last night. *That* can only mean bad things from a plot point of view.

Avantika awoke to arguably more pleasant circumstances—muffled screaming and the distant slamming of a door. She opened her eyes and in the best traditions of fiction, shut them immediately and groaned. She had slept with her contact lenses in, which meant her eyes now felt drier than sandpaper left out in the sun in sub-Saharan Africa. Blinking furiously, she sat up and clutched her spinning head. Another happy side-effect of crossing thirty. Blearily, she conducted a preliminary investigation. Clothes, on; underwear, intact; shoes, neatly lined up by the side of the bed; bag, right next to the shoes; body, in dire need of water, but otherwise unharmed. So far, so boring. Thank God. But—

Room, unfamiliar. She grabbed the bottle of water on the nightstand. Gulping greedily, she proceeded to the next level of journalistic enquiry. The five 'w's and one 'h' variety[1]. Where was she? When did she get here? Who got her here? Why? What was she going to do now? And perhaps most pertinent of all, how much trouble was she in?

She rose to her feet, a little unsteadily—the world seemed to insist on dipping to the right—and made her way to the window, parting the curtains ever so slightly. A lawn dappled with sunlight. And immediately outside the window, a laburnum in full bloom. Something clicked in her head. And suddenly, all the happy ignorance drained from her mind. The bar. The alcohol. Dhruv.

Fuck.

No, that wasn't doing the situation proper justice.

FUCK.

Ah yes, much better.

The night was coming back in needless, relentless flashes now. Laughter. More alcohol. Trying to call an Ola.

---

1 Before cub reporters become cub reporters, they usually go to journalism school where they are taught the basic elements of any news story: What happened? Who did it happen to? Where did it happen? When did it happen? Why did it happen? How did it happen? They forget to mention that if you ask these questions relive and assertively enough, you can make a person relive their childhood without resorting to hypnotherapy.

Calling Shibani by mistake. Giggling over it. Jesus, *giggling.* Dropping the mobile phone. Phone refusing to start. Standing up, quickly followed by falling down. And being caught by … FUCK … Dhruv. So bad, so bad, so bad!

Okay, first things first. She reached into her bag and fished out her phone. When she hit the power button, it started as if nothing had happened, as if last night was just a dream. It might as well have whistled nonchalantly, the bastard. She shot it a look of pure hatred. It pinged happily and told her she had two new messages—one from her phone service provider, urging her to try 4G and the other from her bank, proclaiming her laughable account balance. Along with—Oh! God!—seven missed calls from Aai and Baba!

They were in Bangalore, visiting friends at the moment. And while that meant that they didn't know she hadn't gone home last night, they would nevertheless be worried senseless by now. She hit Aai's number on her speed dial and waited for the call to connect.

'Hello, Aai?'

'Avanti! *Kai hey?* How many times to call you? Are you so busy you can't answer your own mother's call?'

She was angry. Thank God.

'Sorry, Aai … what—'

'What sorry? You know how worried Baba is? He was about to book tickets to come back today!'

'What? No, no—'

'You're not a child anymore. Learn to be more responsible, no?'

'Yes, I'm sorry, but Aai, I was caught up in something serious.'

'Serious? You are alright, no?' This was not a woman prone to hysterics. This was a woman who had taken with infinite calm, her only daughter's decision to enter the world of investigative journalism. While her husband had flapped around, raging about the needless dangers of the profession as compared to say, chartered accountancy, she had simply told her to be careful and to get on with it. Later, she had taken with equal equanimity Avantika's move to feature writing.

But the Nirbhaya rape in Delhi and closer home, the Shakti Mills incident in Mumbai had rattled her more than she cared to admit. The latter, in particular had left her shaken—the survivor had been a young photo-journalist. No, these days were different from those safe, carefree days of ten years ago. This country was barely the same.

'I'm fine Aai, don't worry. It's ... remember Laxmi from my school?'

Puzzled silence on the other end. 'Who?'

'Laxmi,' Avantika repeated, 'She was in my class. We used to go to tuitions together, remember?'

'Oh ... yes, yes.' She could picture her mother's face softening, along with her voice, 'Laxmi ... Swaminathan, wasn't it? How is she?'

Dead. Maybe murdered.

'She ... passed away suddenly ... this week.'

'What?' the shock in her mother's voice was clear, 'Oh God! How?'

Avantika gave her the basics, sparing her the details. Somewhere around college, she had decided that parents, like young children, needed to be sheltered from the harsh reality of this world.

'*Arey-re*, that poor girl,' her mother murmured, 'Her mother ... I ... I can't even imagine—'

'So... basically,' Avantika said, after a moment's silence, 'I was at her place and stuff, so ... that's why, you know, the phone—'

She mentally replayed the sentence. It had all the working parts of a reasonable explanation, but nothing connecting them to add up to a lie. As such. Luckily, her mother hadn't noticed.

'Okay, okay... ,' she murmured, 'I'll tell Baba. You just try to pick up next time, okay? Or at least, call back. He gets worried. You know how he is.'

Avantika rolled her eyes. She knew exactly how much of a drama queen her father could be. Muttering her goodbyes, she hung up. One awkward conversation down, another coming up.

She stared at the door to the bedroom queasily. Maybe she could make a run for it, without anyone noticing. While her head pounded like an amateur drummer. Right. Okay, plan B: winging it. That ought to work. Sure.

Shaking her head in self-disgust, she opened the door slowly and peered outside. Nobody was around. She was about to step out, when a thought struck her. Once she stepped out of this room, she could run into either Aisha or Dhruv, if not both. It was of paramount importance that she not look like a train-wreck when that happened. She took a deep breath and retreated into the room. One glance at the dressing table mirror confirmed her suspicions: someone had snatched her body while she had been asleep. The perpetrator was staring back at her in the mirror - a creature with bloodshot eyes, under-eye bags large enough to take to a weekend in Khandala and hair that could easily be repurposed into fat-free candy floss.

Muttering 'told-you-so's at herself she headed into the bathroom. Someone thoughtful had made sure that there were some basic toiletries in there. She made herself look at least presentable, if not ravishing. Then, after a final glug from the water bottle, she opened the door and let herself out.

It took a second for her to find her bearings, but eventually, she found her way to a large, well-appointed dining room, where she found Dhruv halfway through some scrambled eggs, reading *The Times of India*.

He looked up as she entered and gave her a warm smile.

She cringed.

'Good morning,' he said, getting up and pulling out a chair for her.

'If you insist,' she said and he grinned.

'Hungover? Or just hungry?' he asked.

Avantika realized it was both and told him so. He nodded in the direction of the table.

'I don't know what you eat when you have a hangover, but I read somewhere that eggs and toast is the best. With orange juice, preferably. Something about carbs and energy or whatever. Want some?'

She nodded gratefully.

'You're okay with scrambled eggs, right?'

'Sure.'

'I'd have asked how you like your eggs before telling the kitchen, but somehow I thought you'd say "unfertilised".' He was clearly trying not to smile and failing.

'Ha ha,' she said rolling her eyes. 'I bet you have to fight girls off with a stick.'

Dhruv smiled just as a smartly-dressed bearer entered with a tray piled with scrambled eggs, toast, butter, orange juice and a pot of coffee. Avantika's stomach gave an excited squeal as the man laid it all in front of her, and she served herself, piling her plate with as much grace as she could muster—which, given how ravenous she suddenly felt, wasn't very much.

Dhruv watched her with amusement for a couple of minutes. After the third butter-drenched toast, she slowed down and wiped her lips delicately with her napkin.

'So I'm just going to ask, okay?' she said, not looking at him. 'Just to clear things. We didn't ... nothing actually ... I mean, I didn't—' She looked helplessly at him. 'Well?' she demanded.

'Nothing happened,' he said solemnly. 'You stamped my toe really hard while trying to stand up. Oh, and Aisha went nuts today when I told her that I'd I brought you home. She *really* doesn't like you, does she? But other than that, nothing.'

She stared at him, then quickly glanced at the door, as if expecting a livid Aisha to walk in any second. Dhruv noticed.

'She left,' he said, having a bite of his toast.

'Um... sorry about that,' Avantika mumbled.

'Don't be,' he said with a casual wave of his hand. 'If I knew how much it would piss her off, I'd have brought you home sooner.'

She opened her mouth to say something, then shut it. And opened it again. And realized that there was nothing she could think of saying to that. She shook her head and took a bite of her scrambled eggs. Then, she realized that she did actually have something to say.

'Okay, this is going to sound ungrateful, but ... why are you being nice to me again?'

'Excuse me?'

'You know. Why bring me home, pick a fight with your sister over it and then give me breakfast? Why so nice?'

Dhruv shook his head in wonder, 'So it's true then, no good deed goes unpunished.'

She didn't reply.

'I don't know what to tell you,' he said. 'I guess I'm basically a nice guy.'

She gave him a sceptical look.

'You don't think I'm a nice guy?' he asked, surprised. 'Why not?'

She took a thoughtful bite of her toast and decided that an honest answer was the best and unfortunately, riskiest course of action. She took a deep breath.

'Because you're basically bringing home strange women from the bar, when your ex-girlfriend's body was discovered just a few days ago.'

Dhruv gave her a sharp look. He put the toast he was holding back on his plate and wiped his mouth with a napkin. Playing for time, Avantika thought.

'First of all, this is one time we're talking about. I don't usually bring home ... it's not a habit, okay? And Laxmi and I...' he shrugged. 'We're not even friends anymore. Weren't. We *weren't* friends.'

'No, but she was Aisha's best friend, doesn't that—'

He pushed back his chair and got up, toast half-eaten on the plate. He didn't look angry, but his face wore a guarded expression and the easy affability of the morning was gone.

'You'll have to excuse me,' he said, 'but I have a shoot lined up in half an hour, so—'

'Yeah, I'll push off,' Avantika said, getting up herself. 'Thanks for breakfast and … um, everything.'

He nodded and left without a word.

Avantika made her way to the room where she had woken up, deep in thought. Dhruv's reaction to her answer had been defensive as she'd expected. But there was more to it. He could have laughed off the implication, or felt offended; instead, he had shut down. And then, there was the fumbling over tenses.

Perhaps he was still not used to thinking of Laxmi in the past tense, but that didn't explain the emphasis with which he denied being friends with her. Questions, more questions to add to the ones she already didn't have answers to. As she wore her shoes, her phone pinged. It was a Facebook notification—a friend request from Mahira. She gaped at it, feeling foolish. Here she was, having breakfast with Aisha's brother, when she should've been trying to reach Shweta! She looked up her contacts and found the number she had saved.

As she walked to the door she heard the sound of a car, and through the window saw a sleek black BMW pulling out of the gate. Dhruv sat in the driver's seat, looking grim.

Minutes later as she walked out of the gate, she reflected that it was like the saying said—all the good ones were either married, gay or hiding something.

1997

It was the lunch break. Or as the girls called it, the long recess. One glorious hour of food and games and gossip, with possibly some last minute homework that refused to get done the night before.

You could see it happening all over the school. In the corridors, which were locked during the recess. Inside the assembly halls, which were never locked. And on the playground laid with black tar and lined with trees, under which girls, in groups of three and four were engaged in complex games involving clapping and chanting. One group sang:

Oo-ma Jo-shi ye yeye
My mothershetoldmesixtyyearsago
There came-a la-dy knockingatthedoor
With a ooh, aah, I wantsome baa...

What the 'baa' was remained a mystery, because they were drowned out by another, more pro-establishment group that was yelling on the top of their voices:

Who stole the cookie from the cookieeeshop?
Mr A stole the cookie from the cookieeeshop.
Whome? Yesyou.

Couldn'tbe. Thenwho?
Mr B stole the cookie from the cookieeeshop.

Along the fringes of the playground, a column of hapless ninth standard Blue House girls stomped past, practising marching for the Annual Day parade. In various corners, younger girls sat together, exchanging tiffin boxes and gossip. And in one far corner, away from the rest, Avantika sat alone. A stainless-steel lunch box lay open before her, a twin to the several others you saw around. She pushed up the big brown spectacles that had slipped down her nose and stared at the book that lay open on her lap. This Heathcliff person was clearly mad. Yet oddly attractive. The spoonful of vegetable pulao stayed poised on the way to her mouth. She was about to turn the page, when a shadow fell across it. She looked up.

'Eating alone again, double-battery?'

It was Aisha. In her shadow, as always, stood the rest of her group—Shweta, Mahira and of course, Laxmi. Avantika gave her a brief look and sighed inwardly. She missed the girl. She missed having someone to laugh with, gossip with; hell, even just to talk to about things other than homework and projects. Everything had been more fun with Laxmi around. Now, school was just a series of days to get through somehow.

She didn't let any of this show, of course, because some vestigial survival instinct in her warned against it. High school was a shark tank. If you were going to swim alone, the least you could do was not let your guard down. They smelled your fear, these girls. Give them one chance, and they'd rip your self-esteem to bits. No, she was better off wearing her loneliness as a badge of honour, tempered by scathing wit and if need be, downright rudeness. I don't need you, I don't need *any* of you, I'm just fiiiiine all by myself. She narrowed her eyes at Aisha. Force fields up, she decided.

'Yes,' she said, 'eating alone.'

'Double-battery,' giggled Mahira. 'She called you double-battery!'

Avantika ignored her.

'I guess people just don't like eating with people who say mean things about others, no?' Aisha asked with a sweet smile.

Avantika considered this. She didn't think 'idiot' was a particularly brutal insult. Besides, not knowing that CO^2 stood for carbon dioxide when you were in the ninth standard *was* pretty idiotic. But in this school, that kind of language was just unacceptable. It was the kind of talk that could turn you into a social pariah. Calling a spade a spade was all fine, but it simply didn't do to call an idiot an idiot. Not when it was Mahira. Or in other words, not when it was a friend of Aisha's.

Avantika put her spoon down. She'd been eating alone for two months now. She didn't hate it—there were enough books in the school library to see her through at least another year of alone time. But the power trip was getting irritating. She smiled at the group.

'You know what else they don't like? Arrogant bitches like you.'

There was a chorus of gasps, followed by some rapid murmuring. What the heck? Nobody spoke that way to... anyone!

Aisha blinked.

'Did you just—'

'Did you just call Aisha a ... bitch?' Shweta asked slowly. She looked shocked, but any moment now anger could take over as the lead expression.

Avantika frowned. Damn it. The glasses were slipping down her nose again. In an alternate universe, perhaps all spectacles were born with a sense of dramatic timing. In this universe, they clearly had no such thing. She pushed them back up.

'No,' she sighed. 'I said arrogant bitch. I'll wait, you go look it up in a dictionary, okay?'

'You think you're so clever, no?' Mahira spat. 'Reading books, using big-big words all the time? Knowing words doesn't make you smart, okay? It just makes you a ... a ...' she hunted around for a word.

'Articulate?' Avantika provided, straightfaced. From the corner of her eye, she spotted Laxmi trying to hide a smile.

The murmuring was growing. Girls sitting nearby were turning to look. Some had begun gathering around the little scene, nudging each other and whispering among themselves. Had it been two ordinary girls, one of the school prefects would've showed up by now. But Aisha *was* a prefect. You didn't back-answer prefects. Things were going to get interesting.

Now if this had been a boys' school, someone would be getting pulled by the neck-tie and thrown on the ground right about now. Then there would be some awkward punches thrown, a few kicks here and there, maybe a minor scuffle, till someone gave in and then they'd all shake hands and go back to class. But since that was neither ladylike nor, frankly, half the fun, the girls stuck to what they knew.

A malicious smile crossed Aisha's face.

'Tch, tch, tch, swearing,' she said shaking her head. 'That too in front of a prefect. I think Miss Gomes should hear about this. And then, who knows? Maybe she'll kick you out of the class play and we won't have to see your bad acting.'

Avantika gave her a blank look that didn't betray the sudden panic she now felt. Each class put up a play once in the course of every school year. This year, class IX A was putting up *A Midsummer Night's Dream* for the mid-term school programme and she had bagged the role of Puck. Aisha, with her long silky hair and grey eyes, was playing Titania, the Queen of Fairies. But Avantika didn't mind. She thought Puck was a riot and she enjoyed every minute she played him. Being kicked out of the play would ... hurt.

'Go ahead,' she said nevertheless. 'Good luck finding a replacement at such short notice.'

'Oh that won't be a problem,' Aisha smirked. 'Laxmi, can take the part. Right, Mimi?'

Mimi? Avantika glanced at Laxmi, who looked away. They barely spoke these days. There hadn't been any fight. It had all been very polite. But it wasn't like before. Before, they had been close. Friends. Best friends even. Now, they were ... classmates. One of whom was apparently called 'Mimi' by her friends. Yuck.

Avantika turned her attention back to Aisha.

'She'll overshadow you, if she does,' she told her. 'Your Titania is just...,' she made a face.

She returned to *Wuthering Heights*, only to have Aisha pull it out of her hands. This was a library book. A lovely old edition, with a crimson leather binding and wafer-thin pages that you could bury your nose in and just ... smell. If it tore, it would mean a fine and explaining to Aai and Baba exactly how it tore and begging them to not come to school and complain about bullying. But more importantly, if it tore it meant ... it would be torn. She let go of it without a fight.

Aisha peered at the cover, opened a page at random and read for two seconds.

'Boring,' she said, tossing it back her. 'Just like you.'

Behind her Mahira laughed uproariously, as if a great joke had been cracked.

'You just don't learn, do you?' Aisha said, bending down till she was level with Avantika. 'You think you can just insult me and my friends and I won't do anything about it? I'm *used* to winning, Avantika. I *never* lose. Especially to four-eyed losers like you.'

On cue, Mahira trilled, 'Four-eyed loser, hahaha!'

Avantika looked at the pulao in her tiffin. Aai had made it because she had told her how bored she was of eating chapati-bhaji every day. It was yummy. It would be a shame to waste it. But if she let Aisha get away with this, she'd have to go through more of this. Her gaze fell on her water-bottle, lying innocently next to her tiffin. How much trouble could she get in? Only one way to find out.

She squinted up at Aisha. Then, in one quick motion, she had grabbed her Squeeze-E[2] bottle and squirted all

---

2 The Squeeze-E was a soft, squishy revolution in the age of hard thermos-like water-bottles. It had freezable ice-packs to keep your water cold, came in a range of exciting colours and shapes and made you sway like a pendulum, when slung around your neck.

the water inside it straight on to Aisha's face and eyes. The girl staggered back in shock, stumbled and fell. Involuntary laughter broke out among the girls standing on the sidelines. Avantika was up like a shot, bending down to face her.

'There's always a first time,' she said, with a smile.

Nine

'Where are you?' Uday demanded, over the phone.

'I've ... ah ... just stepped out for some coffee,' Avantika replied.

This was technically true. If 'coffee' could be translated into 'conversation with Shweta in the course of which I hope to get some facts about Laxmi's disappearance'. She had, in fact, considered inviting the woman out for coffee, but had rubbished the plan after thinking about it. Shweta didn't have any reason to agree to a meeting like that. She'd called anyway and hadn't been surprised to have her call cut off. Shweta wouldn't answer calls from strange numbers. For that matter, she probably wouldn't answer Avantika's call even if she did have her number. No, it would have to be an ambush. But a carefully thought-out one.

Which is why right now, she was waiting outside Bhagwanwadi Municipal Hospital's Maternity Ward B[1],

1 Not all are born equal. Some are born in luxurious birthing suites with attached guest rooms. Others are born in maternity wards—one huge room with several women in labour lying side by side on beds, taking turns to dilate their cervices, like the world's most horrifying assembly line. True story.

feeling more out of place than a vegetarian at a bacon breakfast.

The corridor was dingy and painted a toxic shade of pistachio green. Bits of plaster had crumbled from the walls that were lined with surplus relatives, who had been shooed out of wards by irate nurses. One of these nurses had earlier informed her that Dr Shweta Kakkar was conducting her morning rounds, and unless someone suddenly gave birth, would be available to talk in twenty minutes.

Avantika had been a little taken aback by this. Somehow she just couldn't imagine Shweta as an ObGyn. But then, that was doctors for you. Nowhere on their faces did it say what part of the human anatomy was under their supervision. You could talk for hours to a perfectly charming man you met at a party and discover much later that he had been a proctologist[2] all along.

'Really. Coffee.' The disbelief in Uday's voice was quite clear.

'Fine, you got me, I'm actually in Mordor, throwing away the one true ring in the depths of—'

'Shut up. Nathan has been prowling around your desk. Any moment now, he's going to come up to me and ask where you are.'

'Tell him you don't know.'

---

2 Proctologists are probably the butt of all jokes in the medical fraternity. And that's unfair. Because it's a shitty job, but someone's got to do it. They're probably great people, always ready to watch your back and stuff.

'I *don't* know. But I know this—you've been going AWOL pretty often this past week and one of these days Nathan is going to—'

'Yell at me? Make my life miserable? Threaten to fire me? No, wait, he already did *that*—'

'Avanti—'

'I know, I know. Look ... I'm working on something ... important, okay? Once that gets wrapped up, I'll be a good little girl again. Promise.'

There was silence on the other end. When Uday finally spoke, he sounded as if he was trying not to sound worried. 'Whatever it is you're doing... just be careful, alright?' he said. 'If something happens to you ... it's a bitch finding new feature-writers these days.'

She snorted and hung up. Uday could be such an old woman sometimes. She glanced at her watch. She had been standing here for twenty minutes now and the general gloom was getting to her. That, and the woman in the violently purple saree, who was complaining loudly over the phone about how her daughter-in-law had given birth to a daughter again. If Shweta didn't come out soon, she was going to end up doing something to that woman. It would be painful. For the woman. Just then, the door of the maternity ward opened and a very harried Shweta emerged, followed by a few gormless-looking interns. She was wearing the standard white lab coat over a block-printed salwar kurta, which did little to disguise her reed-thin figure. A surgical green cloth mask hung about her neck and her limp hair was pulled back into a tight ponytail, which made her gaunt face seem severe. As she passed by,

Avantika noticed the dark circles under her eyes and the strands of grey in her hair.

'Shweta? Shweta Kakkar?'

Shweta turned around. Avantika waved cheerfully and said, 'Oh my god! What a small world! How *are* you?'

Shweta's eyes narrowed with the effort of recognition and an uncertain smile appeared on her lips. 'Hi... erm—'

'It's me! Avantika Pandit. St Agatha?'

The smile dimmed a bit. 'Oh. Hi.'

'It's so good to see you! Listen, it looks like you're busy but if you have five minutes, I'd love to catch up.'

'Um ... I'm sorry ... I don't think I have time today,' said Shweta with a fake smile.

At which point the most gormless of the interns pushed his rimless spectacles up his nose and squeaked, 'Actually ma'am, we have the next half an hour free.'

Poor guy. Shweta shot him a look of such menace that he positively shrank a few inches. Avantika pretended not to notice. 'Great! How about a quick tea? The canteen is upstairs, right?'

And before Shweta could protest, she linked her arm through hers and began walking away from the interns.

'What are you doing here?' Shweta asked her, trying to wriggle her hand away.

'Oh, I'm doing a story on municipal hospitals in the city. I work at *Mumbai Daily* now. But look at you—doctor and all. So cool!'

Shweta didn't say anything.

'And an ObGyn!' Avantika continued. 'It must be so rewarding no? Bringing children into the world. You must feel so proud!'

'What is your article about?'

'Oh. It's a piece on how despite modern healthcare facilities in the suburbs, a lot of people still come to municipal hospitals, especially teaching hospitals like Bhagwanwadi.'

Which was rubbish, because it wasn't much of a mystery. Municipal hospitals were cheaper. Teaching hospitals, more so, as patients who couldn't afford pricey healthcare were just the sort of willing guinea pigs eager young medical students needed to practice their fledgling skills on. Shweta must've guessed as much, because she gave Avantika a searching look, as if trying to figure out if she was telling the truth. Avantika smiled innocently in response and Shweta looked away.

'This way,' she said, and walked into a large room with off-white doors.

The canteen was done up in the best traditions of government issue decor. There were speckled beige cement tiles on the floor and, in complete and terrible contrast, brilliant white glazed tiles on the walls. White fluorescent tube-lights hung from the ceiling. Rickety tables with formica tops were strewn around in no particular order and each table was surrounded by four or five red moulded plastic chairs.

They picked a table at random and sat down. A canteen boy in a stained khaki uniform approached and Shweta ordered two teas. They came in mismatched ceramic cups—Shweta's had a chintzy floral pattern and a chipped handle, Avantika's bore the remnants of a golden rim and an unreadable crest.

Shweta sipped her tea in silence, while Avantika toyed with hers. 'So... how've you been?' She asked.

'Busy.'

'I'll bet! It must be tough, no? I mean, working in a municipal hospital rather than a private one.'

'Yes.'

'Not like *Grey's Anatomy* then?'

'No.'

Avantika took a sip of her tea. It was orange and loaded with ginger. Probably boiled well past an inch of its life.

'You know who I ran into the other day? Mahira. She's married now. To some bigshot businessman, from the sound of it.'

'Um-hmm.'

'What about you? Have you—'

'Is that really any of your business?'

Avantika blinked. Shweta's face was expressionless but the 'back off' in her words couldn't have been clearer.

'Sorry?'

'It's a personal question, isn't it? If I'm married or not.'

Avantika gave her a wide smile. 'Oh, no, no, no! I was just asking if you've been in touch with anyone from school!'

Shweta looked away and stared out of the window. 'I'm in touch with some friends. Not all.'

'I heard Aisha designs bags now. They're supposed to be really cool.'

Shweta smiled reluctantly. 'She gave me one. It's pretty.'

'Nice. But then, you two were always close.'

Shweta shrugged noncommittally, but Avantika could see that she was pleased.

'What about the rest of your gang? What are they up to?'

Shweta arched her eyebrows, 'You're very interested. Why? It's not like you got along with us back then.'

And what an understatement that was. Avantika waved her hands dismissively. 'Come on, that was so long ago. Who holds on to stuff like that?'

Shweta finished her tea and set her cup on the table. She placed a ten rupee note under it and got up. Looking Avantika straight in the eye, she said, 'I do.'

1998

Avantika got up from the desk she was pretending to play the piano on, and strode over to Shweta. 'How *are* you, my dear Earnest?' she put out a hand, 'What brings you up to town?'

Shweta took a step back with a look of utter distaste on her face. 'Don't be stupid.'

'Now what?'

'We're supposed to be friends. Friends don't shake hands.'

'But Earnest and Algernon—'

'... are friends. Friends hug. Ask anyone. You don't have any friends na, otherwise you would've known.'

Ouch. That hurt. Ever since Laxmi had joined Aisha's gang, she had pretty much been a lone wolf. There were other groups in the class that she could've joined, but their friendships had already been cemented and there was no real place for a newcomer. Particularly one with a bit of a mouth on her. Still, it was probably her motor-mouth that had bagged her the role of Algernon in *The Importance of Being Earnest,* so she didn't think she ought to complain too much about it.

The interschool dramatics competition was coming up and this year, St Agatha's would be putting up an adaptation of Oscar Wilde's immortal play *The Importance of Being Earnest.* She had been so thrilled when she found out. She loved Wilde's characters, Algy in particular. And the writing, the sheer comic genius of the man! It was going to be a blast, despite the fact that Aisha was going to be playing the part of Algernon's sister, Gwendolyn. But then, the headmistress had insisted that Shweta-bloody-Kakkar be cast as Earnest, because apparently she 'was a natural'. Yeah right. More like the old cow was a natural Ruchika Kakkar fan. Shweta's mom.

In her days, Ruchika Kakkar had been the star of the Hindi and English theatre circuits. Her Ophelia left the audience in tears, her Shakuntala moved them beyond words. But a bout of laryngitis had led to complications that severely affected her vocal chords. She lost her voice projection and with it, her future as a theatre actress. Today, Ruchika Kakkar was a respected theatre critic, and her daughter, a royal pain in the ass.

It wasn't just that Shweta believed she knew *everything* about acting. It wasn't just that she believed she was a fantastic actress. It wasn't just that she and Aisha had a made a point of ganging up on Avantika during rehearsals. It was all of it together, that was getting on Avantika's nerves. But she was determined not to let it ruin the rehearsals and the play for her.

'Fine, let's try hugging,' she said, trying to keep the sarcasm in her voice to a minimum, as she walked back to the desk that was moonlighting as a grand piano.

They were rehearsing in the small assembly hall and the rest of the cast were standing on either side of the two desks that served as markers to separate the wings from the rest of the stage. The rest of the set—a Victorian drawing room—would be in place in time for the dress rehearsal. Fifteen seconds later, Shweta's petulant voice rang out again in the near-empty hall.

'No, still wrong! That's not how you hug a *friend*, that's how you hug a *boy*!'

'What?'

'Boys, you nerd. You *have* heard of boys, right?'

Titters broke out amidst Aisha and her minions. As she tried to ignore the laughter, Avantika wondered why Aisha wasn't in the wings with the rest of the cast. She stole a quick look at the girl. Laxmi was sitting right next to Aisha, but she hadn't joined in the giggles. She turned her attention back to Shweta.

'Whatever. Either you show me what you think is the right kind of hug, or shut up,' she said.

Shweta gave an exaggerated sigh and walked over to her. Then she threw her hands around Avantika's shoulders, tilted her own head to the side and rested her palms on Avantika's back. A second later, she pulled away.

'*That's* how you hug a friend.'

'No, that's how *you* hug a friend. Algernon is a man. He wouldn't hug like that.'

'Oh please, like you know what Algernon would or wouldn't do.'

'Why? Why can't I know?'

'Because you don't know anything about guys. You don't even have a guy, right?'

Avantika felt her hands clench into fists. 'Go to hell!'

'What is going on here?,' asked a stern voice.

Miss Shah, their English teacher and the director of the play, had just walked in. A slim woman in her late-thirties with salt-and-pepper hair, she wore a crisp handloom cotton saree and a forbidding expression. The only time her face softened was when she taught the girls poetry. Avantika liked her, both for her love for the language as well as for her no-nonsense approach to life.

Now, her entrance had a dramatic effect on the rest. Girls who had been sitting with their legs stretched out on chairs, immediately adjusted themselves into more demure poses. Casual background conversations stopped. The cast unconsciously stood straighter. Only Aisha remained slouched comfortably in her seat, unaffected and indifferent.

'See no, Miss, I was only telling her she's not hugging properly and she started shouting at me,' said Shweta. 'Earnest and Algernon are supposed to be the best of friends. But how can I can pretend like I'm friends with someone who is so stupid?'

'Why not?' Avantika snapped. 'You have lots of practice, no? Being Mahira's friend.'

There were a few gasps from Aisha's gang, the loudest, naturally from Mahira herself. Miss Shah raised her eyebrows.

'Hawww, Miss!' Mahira called out. 'Did you hear, Miss? Did you hear what Avantika—'

'I heard her, Mahira, I'm not deaf. Avantika ... that was unnecessary. Apologize.'

Avantika stared at her shoes. Her cheeks were burning with rage. Shweta had been baiting her all through the rehearsal and she had finally cracked. She was about to open her mouth to say sorry, when Aisha got up from her seat.

'Miss, I don't think saying sorry is enough. She can't just insult another girl like that. You have to take her out of the play as a punishment.'

Miss Shah looked at her steadily and spoke in a voice that seemed deceptively calm. 'Excuse me?' she said, 'I *have to*? Did someone appoint you headmistress in the past hour, Aisha?'

The girl smiled, in what she must've thought was a winning manner. 'No, Miss. But—'

'Then sit down and stay quiet. Avantika, are you going to apologize?'

'Yes, Miss. I'm ... sorry. I shouldn't have said that.'

Miss Shah nodded.

'Good. Now apologize to Shweta and Mahira.'

Avantika gritted her teeth. Just get it over with, she told herself. You know you shouldn't have said it. It's two words, get them out.

'I'm sorry,' she muttered in their general direction.

Miss Shah clapped her hands twice and said, 'Okay, back to practice. Let's take it from Earnest's entry.'

The rest of the rehearsal continued more or less peacefully, especially after Miss Shah pointed out that gentlemen in the Victorian era were not known for their excessive fondness for hugging. Shweta kept glaring at Avantika between scenes, but behaved herself when they were on stage. Towards the end of the second act however, she lost her patience.

'What is wrong with you?' she yelled. 'Why aren't you getting this line right? You haven't learned your lines, na?'

'I have! But you're going too fast!'

'No! You're going too slow!'

The dialogue in question was supposed to be said together by Earnest and Algernon, in response to a similar chorused line from Gwendolyn and Cecily. Aisha and Reema were managing to say their lines together just fine. Avantika felt a pause was called for after their line, but Shweta clearly didn't share her opinion.

'Miss, see Miss!' she appealed. 'She is hopeless, Miss!'

She glared at Avantika, who met her gaze head-on. Miss Shah looked calmly at the pair of them. 'I'll be the judge of that, Shweta. Let's take the scene from the top.'

'No, Miss, she can't act, she's rude, she keeps arguing! Can't someone else do Algernon's role? Maybe Meenal? She's not *this* bad, Miss.'

A strange look came over Miss Shah's face. 'Meenal, yes,' she said, almost to herself. 'That's not a bad idea.'

Avantika couldn't believe what was happening.

'What are you doing?' she asked Shweta in a furious whisper. 'Why are you doing this to me?'

'Avantika,' Shweta said in the tones of someone trying to explain quantum physics to a turtle. 'We need to win interschool and we can't do it unless we're the best. You want the school to win, na? Then you have to understand.'

Avantika felt like she'd break into tears any moment. Not because she was sad, although she was, but because she was filled with a dark, impotent rage. She clenched her fists and took a deep breath. If she cried in front of Shweta and Aisha, for any reason, they'd win. She turned to Miss Shah, trying to stop her voice from shaking.

'Miss? Should I come down from the stage?'

Miss Shah gave her a puzzled look.

'You're mid-scene Avantika. Don't be silly.'

'But Miss ... you said—'

'Meenal, take over from Shweta, please.'

There was deathly silence and then muttering broke out through the auditorium. Shweta's face turned ashen.

'Miss!' she gasped. 'No!'

She looked frantically at Aisha, who was standing across the stage from her. Aisha nodded and turned to face Miss Shah.

'Miss...,' began Aisha.

'Do you want me to find a new Gwendolyn as well, Aisha?'

Aisha shut up, although she looked like she was just itching to say something.

'The play is in four weeks and we're staging a comedy,' said Miss Shah. 'That means there shouldn't be any drama, onstage or off it. Thank you for the casting suggestion, Shweta. You can step down now. Meenal, take up her position, please.'

As the bewildered Meenal came up on stage, Shweta stormed off, close to tears. But she didn't leave the hall. Instead, she joined the rest of Aisha's clique in the audience, who instantly began murmuring their condolences.

Avantika tried to ignore the venomous glances they were shooting in her direction.

'Avantika. Avantika?' Miss Shah's voice cut through her distraction, 'Let's take it from your entry. Places, everyone.'

Avantika stepped off-stage, passing Aisha as she did so. The girl gave her a cold look and whispered, just loud enough for her to hear, 'You just wait now.'

Avantika simply shook her head. She was getting really tired of these needless mind-games. She went through the rehearsal pretending everything was fine. It wasn't really her fault that Shweta wasn't in the play anymore. And as it turned out, that wasn't a very big drawback for the production. Meenal's comic timing was loads better than Shweta's and she had a good memory for her lines. Besides, her chemistry with Avantika was decidedly less awkward and that showed in their comic give-and-take. Miss Shah nodded approvingly at the end of the rehearsal and was giving both the girls notes on their performance, when Avantika noticed Aisha walking towards Shweta.

The two walked a few steps away from the rest and there was a furious exchange of words, in the course of which Shweta began to look increasingly horrified. At one point, she shook her head frantically, but Aisha held her hands in her own and whispered something to her that made her calm down. They both looked towards Miss Shah and finally, Shweta nodded. Aisha gave her an encouraging pat on the back and walked away. Shweta took a deep breath and walked towards Miss Shah.

'Miss ... can I talk to you alone, please?'

'You *can*. But you *may* not. I have to go to my next class, Shweta, and I'm sure you have to too.'

'Can ... ma ... could ... we talk after school then, Miss?'

Miss Shah gave her a brief glance, as if trying to read her mind. Then she shrugged. 'All right. Come to the 7B classroom when you're done. I'll be correcting papers there.'

Shweta nodded meekly and left. Avantika figured she'd try to butter Miss Shah up, but she didn't see it working. And that was the last thought she had on the matter for a while.

The next few weeks passed in a blur of rehearsals and schoolwork. And the following month, the St Agatha girls proudly lifted the shiny golden trophy for Best Play at the interschool dramatics competition. Miss Shah took her cast out for ice-cream to celebrate and Avantika wished every Friday was as delightful as this one had been.

Her happiness, like all happiness, was short-lived. The following Monday, Miss Shah didn't show up for her usual English class. Her replacement—Miss Hardikar—was brief in her explanation. Miss Shah was on leave. Yes, it was sudden. No, she didn't know when Miss Shah would be back. Yes, maybe it was a family emergency, now could everyone please turn to chapter seven in their textbooks? The girls whispered among themselves and the whispers grew. Miss Shah was ill. No, she was on vacation in Seashells. No, she had eloped with an electrician. One girl went around telling anyone who'd listen that after getting a particularly bad grade in her English unit test, she had wished that Miss Shah would disappear and look, her wish had come true!

But it is the nature of news to travel and the nature of salacious news to travel faster than light, so before the week was out, the news was: Miss Shah had been suspended because a student had complained that she had touched her inappropriately. Gasps went up in the corridors of St Agatha, after all the necessary phrases had been looked up in a dictionary. The poor girl! So scary! But who was the poor girl who had made the complaint? The teachers certainly weren't saying. All that could be said for certain was that Aisha and Shweta couldn't stop grinning these days.

Ten

'Shweta! Wait!'

Avantika ran behind her as Shweta strode down the corridor. 'Look, can't we just get over what happened and—'

Shweta stopped suddenly and turned around. 'You think I'm an idiot? You think I'm going to fall for this whole surprise reunion act you have going on? The only reason I even came to the canteen with you was because I didn't want to make a scene in front of my juniors! I know you're not here for some stupid article, Avantika. So please shut up and go away.'

She began to walk away again. Avantika sighed and followed. 'You're right. I'm not here for a story.'

'Then why are you here? And don't lie.'

'Okay.'

And with that, Avantika gave her a quick recap of the events that had happened since she went to Aisha's house for the interview. 'I have to know what happened to her. I thought ... maybe you know something that ... I dunno.'

Shweta stopped outside a dirty beige door marked 'Radiology—No Entry Without Permission' and turned to face Avantika. 'I know a lot of things you don't. Doesn't mean I'm going to tell you any of them.'

'Shweta, please, this is important. Tell me how you knew it was Laxmi's body in the morgue.'

Shweta's face darkened. 'Oh really? It's important? Guess what? So was that play!'

'Oh come on,' Avantika rolled her eyes. 'Not that again. It was just a bloody play.'

'To *you*! To *you*, it was just a play. To me, it was a chance to show my mother I could act! To convince her to let me become an actress after school!'

Avantika blinked. 'W... what?'

'We had a deal, my mom and I. If I won the Best Actress prize in the interschool competition, she'd help me become an actress. We were talking about me going to Trinity College, London. Do you understand what that means?'

'I... don't—'

'No. You don't. It was the chance of a lifetime. And all I had to do was win that prize. You know, even if I hadn't won it, even if she could've just seen me act, seen how good I was, I'd have had a shot. But I didn't even get the chance to show her.'

'Look ... I'm sorry ... but—'

'Are you? Why? Don't be!' Shweta gestured at the dirty corridor with a bitter smile. 'Look where I am today! And it's all thanks to you!'

She pushed open the door to the radiology room and slammed it behind her without another word.

Avantika stood there, looking at the closed door for a few seconds. Then she pinched the bridge of her nose and shook her head wearily. Suddenly, she felt tired. Tired of running around behind people she thought she had left behind in the past. Tired of being polite to people she didn't want to be polite to. And tired of running against dead ends everywhere. She sighed and began walking away from the door. Behind her, someone was shouting.

'Medum! O, Medum!'

A few seconds later, she felt someone brush against her purse. A middle-aged ward boy had sidled up next to her, his khaki uniform stained in places with betel-nut juice.

'How much to call you, Medum?,' he said in Hindi.

'What happened?' she asked in the same language.

He lowered his voice.

'You were saying something about the morgue?'

She looked around. There was only one man sitting on a bench at the far end of the corridor. He appeared to be dozing, his head against the wall.

'I needed some information about a body.'

The ward boy scratched his ear and gave her an appraising look.

'You are Dr Shweta's friend?'

Avantika sized the man up. He was of average height and had the wiry built of someone who eats little and does a lot of manual labour. Under his khaki cap, his hair was hennaed orange, but the orange was flecked by grey. She hadn't seen him in the corridor while she was talking to Shweta, but then, she had been too preoccupied to notice. She decided he must've heard enough of their conversation, to form his own conclusions. Their tones, if not the language, must've been illuminating enough.

'No,' she said.

He grinned, revealing tobacco-stained teeth in various stages of decay. 'Me also,' he said, 'But still I will help you. For Gandhiji.'

Avantika frowned. Gandhi? People still did things in his name? The man noticed the confusion on her face and clarified.

'Gandhiji, medum. Anything anyone does in this country, it's for him only.'

She must've looked utterly clueless at this point because the man actually laughed. 'Arrey what, medum? Whose face is printed on a hundred rupee note, haan?'

It was filthy behind the hospital. Avantika covered her nose and mouth with a tissue and waited impatiently among the discarded syringes, IV drips, half-empty strips of pills and other hospital refuse.

There was an unpleasant smell around the place, part chemical, part organic. If you had to come up with an exact equation, it was probably one part expired paracetamol, three parts human urine, but concentrated and amplified till it felt like it was all you would be able to smell, now and forever. But maybe she was being overly sensitive. Maybe you just had to get used to it. Like the two young ward boys who were leaning against the hospital wall a few feet away from her. They didn't seem to mind the stench, but the foul-smelling beedi they were sharing probably out-stank every other odour. Every couple of minutes they glanced her way, with expressions of curiosity mingled with half-concealed lechery.

She wondered if doing this in the morgue would've been less icky. But Ganesh, the ward boy—and it struck her as ridiculous that a middle-aged man should be called a boy—had insisted she wait here.

'Nobody will say anything, medum, but why to take chance?'

So she waited, checking Facebook on her phone and trying to ignore the fact that her last meal had been the gingery tea with Shweta. Ganesh came out of a side entrance a little while later, empty-handed, not looking even slightly furtive. Her heart sank. He didn't look directly at her, but instead, shot an authoritative look at two ward boys.

'What, you don't have work or what? Get inside!' he barked.

The two shot him insolent looks, but one extinguished the beedi against the wall and put the dog-end behind his ear. Avantika watched them leave, whispering to themselves and sniggering humourlessly behind Ganesh's back.

'You didn't find the file?'

Ganesh made a sound that was presumably a laugh.

'File? For unclaimed body? That also in government hospital? This is not America, medum.'

He pulled out two folded off-white papers from his pocket and handed them to her. Avantika unfolded them to find two identical letter-sized morgue forms, with headings in English and Marathi.

'There were two bodies last month that nobody came for,' Ganesh said, scratching his neck. 'Dr Shweta asked about one of them. I don't know exactly which one so I got both forms.'

Each form had a space for the attending doctor's name. She could just about make out the word 'Kakkar' in the loopy signature on one of them. She frowned. How could an obstetrician double up as a forensic pathologist? One job involved birth and yes, okay, sometimes death. And yes, ObGyns must be dab hands at stitching people up, what with all the C-sections they perform. And it *was* a government facility, but there still had to be *some* protocol, right? Even here, in the Hospital of Horrors, there must be some *rules*, right? She turned to the other form. And frowned.

'There is no signature,' she said, more to herself than to Ganesh, who heard anyway.

'What?'

'Here,' she held out the form. 'Shouldn't there be a sign, from the doctor who did the post-mortem?'

Ganesh gave her a wary look, then looked around casually. Avantika reached into her purse and pulled out a five-hundred-rupee note. She folded it deliberately and put it in the pocket of her jeans. Ganesh's eyes followed it, then rose to meet hers.

'Doctors are busy people, medum,' he said, rubbing the back of his neck. 'They don't always have time for these things.'

'These things meaning signing forms?'

'Sometimes dirty jobs are left to those who are used to doing dirty jobs.'

'Dirty jobs like—?'

He gave her a blank stare.

'Cleaning vomit, washing bedpans, mopping blood in operation theatres, changing bedsheets that patients have crapped on, opening up patients nobody has claimed—'

Avantika felt queasy. She took a deep breath and held out the form with Shweta's scrawl.

'This one has Doctor Shweta's sign, though. How come?'

Ganesh looked beadily at her. 'So many questions you are asking, medum. How come?'

Avantika thought fast. She could always lie, make up some stuff about a personal vendetta against Shweta. That would probably go down well. Or she could tell just him she worked for a newspaper. Would that spook him out? Him, a man who had seen more blood and gore than the props department of the *Saw* franchise?

'I'm a reporter,' she said, watching his face. 'And I think this person,' she pointed to the form, 'may have been my friend.'

Ganesh's face had taken on a guarded expression at the mention of the word 'reporter'. Now he sneered.

'So many friends of one girl? Dr Shweta also said this only. To the Dean. She said this is my very good friend, I don't want anyone else to do post-mortem. Special request and all.'

'And he just *let* her?'

'*She*, medum, *she*,' Ganesh smirked. 'Dean is also woman. And you must be knowing what women are like, no? All emosanal they get.'

Avantika bit back a response and turned her attention back to the forms. She smoothed it out against the wall next to her and held it there. With her other hand, she took a picture of it on her phone. It had a 5 megapixel camera. She could've printed out these photos if she wanted.

'How did she know?' she asked.

'What medum?'

'How did Dr Shweta know that the body was her friend's? Was there some ID?'

Ganesh looked worried.

'Must've been, no? Otherwise how? I remember that body, the face was all... ,' he made a face. 'Nobody wanted to touch it also.'

She handed the forms back to Ganesh with the five-hundred-rupee note discretely tucked inside it[1].

'Thank you for your help,' she said. 'If I need more information—'

He rattled off a ten-digit mobile number, which she duly saved.

'I'll be here only, medum. I know this place inside and outside, every corner, I know. What all goes on, you ask me, I'll tell everything. Gandhiji always said to tell the truth, no?'

And then, with one last sneer for the road, he was gone.

Half an hour later, Avantika was wolfing down a piping hot idli and sambar at an Udipi restaurant down the road. The sambar was thick and tangy, the idlis fluffy and fresh. She ordered a filter coffee to wash them down with and looked around. It was well past lunchtime so most of the tables were empty, except for the one in the

---

1 Anybody who had ever driven a vehicle in Mumbai is well-versed in the fine art of bribery. One does not simply flash money at traffic cops after being pulled over. They are not nautch-girls. You fold a hundred-rupee note twice or thrice, then slip it under your driving license when you hand it over for inspection. This works nearly every time unless you chance upon an honest traffic cop a.k.a one who refuses to understand the subtext of the words, "Saheb, can't we reach some kind of ... compromise?"

corner, where a couple huddled over a gigantic Mysore masala dosa.

As she waited for her order to arrive, she looked at the picture of the morgue form, zooming in to read it better. It had the barest details. The body had been brought in on 15 November by the cops, who'd found it washed up by the Mahim creek. Personal effects were listed as blue jeans, yellow t-shirt, innerwear, a single brown shoe, a black leather wallet and a ring. There were no suspicious bumps on the head, no signs of a struggle on the body, no traces of poison in the system. Cause of death: asphyxia due to aspiration of fluid into air passages, caused by submersion in fluid. Diagnosis: consistent with drowning.

Could Laxmi swim? She couldn't remember. But even if she was a halfway decent swimmer, all it would take was a combination of a deceptively low tide, followed by strong currents to turn even a stroll into the sea into a fatal mistake. The young and the terminally stupid discovered this fact every year at the city's infamous Aksa Beach. But what would Laxmi be doing strolling into the sea, in the first place? The sea, Avantika had read somewhere was a bad place to die. Not that there were any good places to die, but still.

She did a quick Google search on her phone and her expression darkened. It was a slow death, drowning. It could take up to eight minutes, a short time by ordinary standards, a lifetime—literally—while the water is slowly filling your lungs.

She read on, feeling increasingly depressed. In India, one website told her, drowning was the most common form of suicide, especially among women. Another informed her that in the case of homicidal drowning, there were usually signs of strangulation or severe blows to the head. But if a person was rendered helpless or defenceless through alcohol or drugs, and the head was submerged for five to ten minutes even in shallow water, then drowning would occur without any traces of violence. She glanced at the morgue report. There was no mention of either drugs or alcohol in it. What if Shweta had found some in Laxmi's system and not mentioned it in the report? But why would she do that? They were friends.

She turned back to her phone. On a forensic pathology site she found the process of autopsy in cases of drowning. It was described in clinical terms, with words like centrifuged and supernatant, but unfortunately for her, she could guess the meaning, given the context, and imagine it in graphic detail. A wave of nausea rose in her and she hurriedly switched to another website. This one told her that in India, a drowned body could stay afloat for twelve to eighteen hours in the summer and eighteen to twenty-four hours in winter. It went on to add, without warning, that the process loosens the skin and nails and the skin of the hands and legs could be peeled off like a stocking after two to four days of this. She shuddered and shut the site with a decisive tap.

The waiter disturbed her train of thought, as he kept a classic Madras-style steel davarah and tumbler, filled with foamy filter coffee before her. She took a sip—much too hot—and swallowed hurriedly. Pouring a little of the coffee into the wide davarah, she waited for it to cool.

Her father had taught her that. They had gone to pick up admission forms from Ruia College and he had taken her to Mani's Lunch Home and taught her how to cool a bit of the coffee in the davarah, then pour it back into the tumbler, so the temperature averaged out to just the right degree of hot. And thinking of him, she remembered Laxmi's father. Tall, dark, imposing. An authoritative voice, that would ring out in every PTA meeting. A disapproving face that would soften as he sat in the audience during every school play Laxmi was in. And an invisible force that slammed drawers and banged cupboards shut in his room, even as Aunty told them in hushed tones to study quietly because Uncle was "a little tense today".

Avantika thought of him lying silent and speechless in shock and felt her breath catch in her chest. She dipped a finger in the cooling coffee. That should do. She poured it back into the tumbler and took a sip. Perfect. Now, back to the highlights.

Laxmi had drowned. Had she gone into the sea alone or was someone, let's say, the mysterious Ajay, with her? Did she drown or was she drowned? Was she alive when she stepped into the waves in the first place? Avantika bit her lip. And why was there a wallet on her? It must've had something that made Shweta identify her. What was it? A picture, perhaps? Was it important? And what woman carried a wallet on her person? How did one even do that? Shoved in the back pocket, like a man? Or awkwardly in the front pocket?

She knew no women who did that, but all right, let's say it's an eccentricity. Was there money in the wallet? If there wasn't, maybe Laxmi was mugged and killed. But no, that didn't make any sense. If she was mugged, why would they put her wallet back in her pocket? No, strike that. So that left her with ... what? Nothing. Nothing except questions she still couldn't answer. She pulled out Laxmi's diary and rifled through the pages. There were no diary entries as such, just page after page of passionate, heartfelt, slightly corny poems. Here was one:

What is it, they say
Who is it, they ask
Hiding our love, darling
Is the easiest task
For look where they may
Try as they might
They'll never think to find
what's hidden in plain sight.

Okay. The rhyme was a little ... childish, frankly. But hiding your love from the world wasn't very uncommon. If you were certain your parents wouldn't approve of your boyfriend, then not telling them about him was probably a wise move. Especially in a country where an entire village could spontaneously burn a couple alive for the shameful act of falling in love without their parents' or community's permission. Not that Laxmi would have faced any such thing. Her father was pretty strict, but Avantika didn't think he'd go to such extremes.

So, Laxmi was dating someone—presumably this Ajay character—and her parents didn't approve of him or wouldn't have, if they found out about him. But they must've known him. Known of his existence, in any case. What else could 'hiding in plain sight' possibly mean? But exactly how inappropriate was he, for Laxmi to hide the affair from her parents in the first place?

Different caste? Different religion? Different political views, but no, surely that was more of an American thing? Nobody in India cared *that* much about politics. Sure, they cared enough to out-type each other on social media, but in real life, one did tend to look upon those with strong political beliefs with a little pity. Indian politics was ... Indian politics. Any new government, any new party, would slowly become just like its predecessors. First the victims, then the champions of the same, rusty old system. Meet the new boss, same as the old boss, as The Who put it.

But Laxmi had been an Indian woman over thirty. One would think her parents would dance for joy if she married just about anyone. Avantika knew her own parents would probably throw a party, or more realistically a Satyanarayan pooja[2], the day she announced she was going to get hitched. But what if marriage wasn't on the cards for Laxmi? What if it could never be on the cards and *that* was the reason she was keeping the whole thing a secret? Could Ajay already be married perhaps? Unwilling to leave his wife? What if he had decided *not* to leave his wife and had decided to break up with Laxmi and Laxmi had refused to be disposed of so

---

2 A Satyanarayan pooja is like a keg party for Maharashtrians. Just replace the beer with sooji halwa and a keg-stand with lying prostrate before the Lord. Avantika has been formally banned from attending such poojas in the homes of friends and family since the day she had chanted "When you're happy and you know it, do a pooja' during an aarti* at an aunt's place. *The playlist for times when you're trying to be devout. Or at least *appear* devout anyway.

easily and he had decided to dispose her off, the terminal way? Avantika thought about the girl she knew in school. That girl didn't seem likely to do any of this stuff. But that was a long time ago. People change, don't they? Maybe Laxmi had too.

Avantika drummed the table-top impatiently. She was trying to think dispassionately about this, but all she had so far were dead ends that stopped at Ajay. He was the key. She had to find him, or at least, find out *something* concrete about him, before she could get any answers. She gulped down the rest of the coffee. In her mind's eye, she saw a smiling girl with serious eyes and a long, black braid—her legs dangling playfully, as she sat on top of her desk during the big recess. 'An ant walks up to an elephant and whispers something to him,' Laxmi said wide-eyed. 'The elephant laughs and laughs and laughs. What did the ant say to him?' And without waiting for an answer, she grinned. 'I'm pregnant and it's yours!'

Avantika sighed and called for the bill. In her mind, Laxmi laughed, a clear ringing laugh brimming with joy. She paid the bill and left.

Eleven

'Avantika! How nice to see you! I had no idea you still worked here.'

Nathan was looking cheerily at her over the top of his spectacles. Avantika bit back a reply and gave him a tight smile. Beside her, Uday shifted in his seat. His prediction had come true the day before. Nathan had called her into his cabin and given her a high-octane yelling, featuring words like responsibility, absenteeism, work ethic and her personal favourite, not acting like a senior reporter.

'You have what, ten years of experience?' he had barked. 'Shouldn't it show somewhere?'

And he was right. All this amateur detective work she was doing, it was on his time. She was managing to finish the work assigned to her, but that didn't excuse running away from office every time a brainwave popped up. She had tried making up stuff about how she was working on an interesting news story, but he hadn't been in any mood to listen. And now he was bringing things up in the edit meeting! And giving her an opening, in the process. She took a deep breath.

'Yes, sorry about that. I … I've been chasing a story and—'

'Story? No, no, you mean a feature, don't you?'

'Erm, no—'

'Are you sure? Because that's what we pay you for, I thought. Ten filters you *have* to have on your Instagram? Home Remedies for Monsoon Maladies? The Five Best Burgers in Bombay … sorry, Mumbai. No?'

She took another breath. No, she was on the back foot today. Sarcasm wouldn't be a wise move. 'I mean a news story. The kind Uday writes.'

Uday gave her a 'Why are you dragging me into this?' glare, just as Nathan turned his attention to him. He smiled pleasantly and several people in the room were instantly terrified.

'Ah, yes. Uday. And did Uday know you were, how did you put it? Chasing a story?'

'No. Nobody knew.'

'And you didn't feel the need to … oh, just for the fun of it, tell someone?'

'I should have. I'm sorry. It won't happen again.'

Nathan's smile slid off his face a little. He gave Avantika a deeply suspicious look, which she returned with a totally blank one of her own. His eyes narrowed, as if daring her to expose her contrition for the façade he knew it was. She looked downward and said nothing.

'Hmm,' he said, a little thrown by her docility, 'make sure it doesn't.'

She nodded without looking up. The meeting began for real and Nathan got busy handing out assignments.

Avantika thought she could see a pattern now. If someone looked like they were having a good time, they were instantly given a story they were sure to hate covering. If they protested, they were given a similar story the next week. If they didn't, they got something more in keeping with their own interests and talents. She had always wondered why Uday got the most interesting stories to cover and for the first time since joining, it struck her that she'd never seen him complain about an assignment. He had covered with equal equanimity the sanitation workers' strike and the Titwala[1] Flower Show. And in return, he had received without asking, the chance to cover the Sion murder case and before that, the sensational daylight robbery of the State Bank of Rajasthan, by two teenagers armed only with a carrot and a stick.

She confessed her suspicions to Uday after the meeting. He shrugged. 'Never thought about it. Maybe you've got a point.'

He sank into his chair and opened a Google search page on his computer. She sat next to him, at her own desk, drumming her fingers on the keyboard, but not really typing anything. 'But you *do* get the meaty stories. And you never complain, if you're given the shitty ones.'

'Food and crap in the same breath. You have a special gift.'

'Oh, big talk from the fancy journalist! With me you'll say stuff like that, but if tomorrow Nathan tells you to

---

1 A station on the Central Railway line, known for its famous Ganesh temple. Why? What did you think?

cover, I don't know, the Annual General Body Meeting of ... the Lokhandwala Out-of-Work Actors Union—'

'I'll cover it. That's my job.'

She pursed her lips and rounded on him, 'Don't tell me you enjoy that kind of stuff!'

He shrugged, not taking his eyes off the monitor. 'What's there to enjoy or not enjoy? I'm writing something that's true. Something that some people find interesting. And above all, something that is important to people. In this case, the brave men and women who hang out at the Lokhandwala Café Coffee Day at all hours, in full make-up, in case Karan Johar happens to drive by.'

He lowered his voice and leaned in conspiratorially.

'And tomorrow, if I'm doing a story involving Bollywood, I can call up my friend, the Chairman of the Lokhandwala Out-of-Work Actors Union, who is bound to know people, who know people who know someone who was *there* when it happened.'

She shook her head in amazement. 'You opportunistic ass,' she said.

He puffed on an imaginary cigar and said in an immaculate Sean Connery impression: 'Take notsh, kid, take notsh.'

'And here I thought you were all noble and ethical,' she said, rolling her eyes.

'Those are tricky words for someone in our profession, babe. I mean, we have to make choices other people don't. If I have a source who tells me the current location of Dawood, for instance, what do I do? If I print it, he knows we know and makes a run for it. If I tell the police, how do I know I'm telling an officer who's not corrupt? If I tell the

Home Minister and he ends up sending guys to pick up the man, I have still not done what I'm supposed to, which is print the news because my first duty is to my readers.'

Avantika held out a hand to stop him. 'I feel like I'm back in the Ethics in Journalism lecture with Rangachari. It is because of crap like this that I quit proper reporting, you know.'

'No, you quit because it was the easy thing to do.'

'Hey! That is not—'

'Avanti, it's okay. You don't have to justify your decision to me. I know it's easy to get disillusioned with the system and its flaws and loopholes, because God, there are so many of them.' He ran a hand through his hair, rumpling it in the process. 'What happened with you, it's depressingly common. Hell, at least ten people from our batch in college have quit their jobs with newspapers and TV channels and switched to something less ... sapping.'

She looked at him, silent for a moment. 'Then why do *you* do it?' she asked. 'How can you still go on reporting when you know that half the things you write about won't change anything, and the other half will get drowned in procedural nonsense?'

He looked embarrassed. 'You'll think it's daft.'

'Probably. But tell me anyway.'

'It's about starfish. See, one day—'

At which point, obeying the ancient laws of narrative irony, Shibani flounced between them, waving an A4 sheet of paper.

'Is he going with her?' she asked Avantika. 'Has he said something to you?'

Avantika threw up her hands and looked blank, the universal sign for 'Say what?'

'Dhruv!' Shibani exclaimed. 'Is he going to the U.S. with his sister? Because he still hasn't turned in that photography piece!'

'We were talking, you know,' Uday said conversationally.

Shibani turned to him. 'Yes,' she said. Then turning back to Avantika, she went on, 'Also, did he say when he's free to meet me for drinks? Because I called him? And he didn't answer?'

Avantika shook her head again, and held Shibani by the arm. 'I have no idea what you're talking about, Shib.'

Shibani made an impatient sound. 'Dhruv? Juneja? His sister? Aisha? The designer? She has a show in LA in two weeks. Her PR people sent out this release,' she said, holding out the paper in her hand. 'Probably to boost sales here,' she added. 'It makes such a difference, no? Knowing that a designer is selling in the States also.'

Ignoring Shibani, Avantika skimmed through the press release. Aisha was going to have a trunk show at the W Hotel in San Francisco next week. Reps from Macy's, Sears and JC Penney were expected to attend. It was a high-profile event, to be certain, perhaps the most important in Aisha's career so far. A part of her wondered how Aisha would deal with the pressure of such an event, with Laxmi's death so fresh in her mind. People move on, another part of her said, they look forward. After all, how long can you mourn one dead friend? How long do you let her death be a factor? She couldn't speak for Aisha. They were both very different people. Happily oblivious to all this, Shibani prattled on.

'I'm sure she'll do well there. I mean, have you *seen* her latest collection? It's *insane*! Literally *insane*!'

'Literally?' Uday asked, straightfaced, 'It's suffering from a mental disorder?'

But Shibani was in a different world now, one inhabited solely by Aisha's handbags. 'They featured a few pieces in this month's *Vogue* and ermagawd, Avantika, they're so gorge! There was this one bag? With a huge sunflower print? I nearly drooled all over the page! And so ... unique, the sunflowers were all blue? I mean, you never find a yellow bag in any of her collections, but can you imagine? Blue. Sunflowers. I just *had* to take a picture, see?' She whipped out her mobile phone and brandished it at Avantika. 'But it must be damn expensive, you know? Because they had written "price on request" and nobody says that unless it's a very pricey thing?'

Avantika looked up from the press release. She felt a strange sense of disquiet, the kind you get when you're standing on the edge of a precipice and looking down. There is a quiet certainty that things could go terribly wrong any moment, if only you took a step ahead. But that is nothing, mere background noise drowned out by a clear voice in your head telling you what a great idea it was to take that step.

Wordlessly, she took the phone from Shibani's hand. On the screen, a small purse with a print, of yes, blue sunflowers. She zoomed in to the handle. A second later, she gasped.

'I know, right?' Shibani said happily, 'You think Dhruv could get me a discount? I mean he's her brother and he's working here and I'm practically his boss so—'

'Shibani. Fuck off.'

Shibani gave her an affronted look. 'God, Avantika, how rude!'

'Sorry, yes ... now, could you please go away? I need to think.'

As Shibani walked away in a huff, Avantika took a deep breath and sat down very, very slowly on a chair. She didn't want to say or do anything to dislodge the idea that was forming in her head. Sunflowers. Of course. She didn't realize her mouth was open, but she must've looked strange sitting there unblinking, because Uday was giving her a very concerned look.

'You okay?'

She nodded.

'Your eyes have gone very wide. Are you sure you're fine?'

She let out a breath and blinked a few times. Her head was spinning. Sunflowers. Jesus fucking Christ.

'Fine, fine,' she whispered, raising her fingers to her lips, 'I'm an idiot.'

1991

Avantika poked her head out of the wings and stared. So many people! The school auditorium was brightly lit and filled with parents and students and teachers, all sitting in their seats chatting and laughing, waiting for the show to start. And in just a few minutes, she'd be on the stage, facing all of them. The thought made the inside of her stomach wriggle. She gulped and scanned the crowd for Aai and Baba. They had to be somewhere out there, they had dropped her backstage just half an hour ago, but no, she couldn't spot them.

She looked at her costume. A bright yellow sunflower face with a green unitard and green gloved hands for leaves. She was supposed to wave every time the 'All We Need Is Love' bit came in the song. They had practised in every lunch recess for the past month, but she still felt a little nervous. Maybe not a little. Oh no, now she had to go to the toilet.

Scurrying about in her green socks, she went to find her class teacher, Miss Bharucha, to ask her where the toilets were. She found her in one of the dressing rooms behind the stage, strapping on a pair of cardboard wings to Archana Anand, who was dressed as a sparrow. They were surrounded by half of class 3A, all of whom were dressed as assorted birds, animals, trees and clouds.

'Hold still,' Miss Bharucha was telling Archana, 'I have to do five other birds after you.'

'Miss, miss,' Avantika said, tugging at her saree.

'What?'

'Miss, I have to go to the toilet, Miss.'

'Now? The curtain will open in five minutes, Avantika!'

'Miss, please, Miss!'

Miss Bharucha looked heavenward in despair. She had five pairs of wings to strap on, a missing sunflower to replace and a tree with a sudden case of hiccups. This was not turning out to be a very good afternoon.

'Okay, but make it quick,' she said, before pointing Avantika towards the toilet and warning her thrice to hurry up, not lose her way back and not soil her costume on the toilet.

Avantika padded off in the direction Miss Bharucha had pointed in. The toilets were a long way from the stage, away from the dressing rooms and the backstage area. She passed the props and sets of the plays the older classes would put up after theirs, some of their cast practising lines to each other and a few hassled-looking teachers. Everything loomed and in the semi-darkness, she bumped into a number of people, leaving one of her petals looking quite rumpled in the process.

Finally, she found it. A clean whitewashed room with speckled tiles, a giant mirror on one wall and three toilet cubicles. There was someone inside one of them, so Avantika went into the one next to it. She had just about finished and was feeling very pleased with herself for not getting anything on her costume, when she heard the sniffling. It appeared to be coming from the cubicle next to hers.

Cautiously, she stepped out of the cubicle and washed her hands in the basin. The sniffling continued. Avantika didn't know what to do. Miss Bharucha had asked her to hurry back. But someone was crying in there.

'Girlie?' she asked cautiously, 'Why're you crying? Don't cry.'

There was silence for a moment. Then a voice, a very familiar voice, said:

'A... Avantika?'

It was Laxmi! But what was she doing crying inside the toilet? She was also in the show. She should be getting ready right now.

'Laxmi? Why're you crying? You're scared or what?'

'N... no. Y... yes. N... not like that.'

'I'm also a little scared. It's okay. Don't cry.'

More sobbing. Avantika looked at the door to the toilet. Miss Bharucha would be so angry if she was late. But Laxmi would be late too. They'd both get punished! No, no, she had to do something.

'Laxmi, Bharucha Miss said the curtain is going to go up in five minutes. Please come out.'

'N… o! I'm… not coming… out!' Laxmi was sobbing now.

'Are you scared of going on the stage? My mother said, when the curtain goes up, they switch off all other lights and you can't see the people sitting in front of you.'

'I'm… not scared… of the stage!' Laxmi whimpered, 'I don't want to come out because Miss Bharucha says I have to be a sunflower!'

Avantika was confused. What was so bad about being a sunflower? Okay, it was hard to remember when to wave your hands, but it was nothing to cry about. She knew how to help Laxmi with that.

'Don't worry, I'm also a sunflower no,' she said. 'I'll tell you when to wave your hands.'

'I don't want to be a sunflower! They're… y… ye… *yellow*!'

There was a fresh bout of weeping, this time with loud, gasping sobs.

'So?' Avantika asked. 'You don't like yellow colour or what?'

She waited for an answer but there was only silence. She put her ear to the door of the cubicle.

'Tell me no. What happened? I'm your friend, na?'

Then a very small, terrified voice whispered from the other side:

'I'm… afraid… of it.'

Avantika blinked. She felt like laughing. Afraid of yellow? How can anyone be afraid of a colour? How dumb. Shee. Anything, Laxmi was saying.

'Why are you afraid of it?', she asked, 'It doesn't ... do anything to you.'

'I know ... but I'm still scared,' Laxmi's words sounded muffled. As if whatever she was feeling was too big to fit into them. 'Every time I see something yellow, my stomach feels funny and I can't breathe. I can't go near it. I can't touch it. I can't be a sunflower. I can't, I can't, I *can't*!'

And with that, she started crying so badly, Avantika's own stomach felt funny. She felt like running and finding a grown-up and telling them everything so they could help Laxmi. But if she went near the stage right now, Miss Bharucha would just push her on the stage without listening to anything she had to say. That's what grown-ups did. They never think that you could have anything important to say to them. They never listen. No, grown-ups wouldn't be able to help. She would just have to manage on her own.

'Don't cry, Laxmi. Please don't cry?' she said. 'You don't have to be a sunflower. If Miss Bharucha can't find you, then she can't make you a sunflower.'

Laxmi's sobs turned into sniffles as she seemed to consider this. Encouraged, Avantika continued. 'You wait here only. Don't go out. Once our show is over, I'll ... tell Miss Bharucha I have to do number 1 again. Then I'll come back here and take you outside. You tell her ... you tell her you got lost. You couldn't find the stage. Okay?'

She heard Laxmi blowing her nose on a hanky. 'O... okay.'

'Okay, bye. I'll come back quickly, okay?'

Avantika turned to leave, when she heard Laxmi call out from the cubicle.

'Avantika?'

'What?'

'You won't tell anyone, no? How I'm scared of ... that colour?'

'No, no.'

'Godpromisemotherswear?'

'Godpromisemotherswear.'

A couple of minutes later, a frantic Miss Bharucha saw Avantika get in line behind the two other sunflowers and heaved a sigh of relief. 3A's dance performance to *All We Need Is Love* by The Beatles was declared a massive success by the audience. Critics claimed that an additional sunflower would've added some extra zing to the proceedings, but it was generally felt that the hiccupping tree made up for it, as a subtle symbol of the director's postmodernist angst.

Twelve

Avantika sped down Lamington Road on her scooter, her head buzzing. Laxmi had been terrified of the colour yellow. She had to find out if the phobia had continued into adulthood, because if it had, then it could only mean one thing: the body that had been discovered, that had been cremated, the body that was wearing a yellow t-shirt, wasn't Laxmi's. And if she was right about the other thing she'd discovered ... but no, that was just conjecture at this point.

She pulled into Laxmi's lane and parked amidst the row of bikes outside her building. Racing up the stairs, she considered what she was about to do. It wasn't exactly what you'd call a masterplan. But still, she had to give it a shot.

She rang the bell of the Swaminathan residence. A few moments later, Laxmi's mother opened the door.

'Oh—'

'Hi, Aunty—'

'Come in, come in, what a surprise—'

Avantika followed her inside, refusing her offer of coffee, and smiled in resignation when the woman ignored her protests and brought out a cup of filter coffee anyway. She sipped it in silence for a moment, while Laxmi's mother sat on the sofa next to her, quiet and unsure.

'You must be wondering why...' she said, just as Laxmi's mother asked, 'So what brings you—'

They both smiled awkwardly.

'I came to see how you're doing, Aunty,' Avantika replied.

Laxmi's mother smiled sadly, a smile that was three-fourths a sigh.

'I'm ... better than before. I don't really know ... if I can be better than this now.'

Avantika kept down her mug on a side table next to the sofa. 'When I told my mother what had happened, she was quite ... shaken. I think a part of her must've imagined what it would be like if something like that happens to me.'

'It is a terrible blessing, you know, being the mother of a daughter,' Laxmi's mother sniffed, 'your heart is filled with so much happiness. But it is *always* mixed with fear. Your whole life you spend waiting, scared, that one day, something bad, something *horrible* will happen to your baby girl. How could it not? How could something so beautiful, so precious be given to you for nothing? How can this much happiness not have a price?' Her voice caught for a moment. 'Your mother is lucky. She has not had to pay it.'

Avantika put a hand over hers and gave it a comforting squeeze. Laxmi's mother gasped, as if willing herself not to cry. Her lower lip quivered. Avantika shook her head, hating herself for what she was about to do.

'I'm sorry, Aunty,' she began. 'But I was ... I wanted to ask you something.'

'What?'

'Laxmi's phobia of yellow—'

The woman gave her a startled look. 'You knew?'

'Yes ... she told me when we were in school.'

'We had told her not to tell anyone. *We* never talked about it. You know how people are ... her father was worried she wouldn't get any good marriage proposals.'

Avantika swore inwardly. Fucking marriage proposals. If you were a young Indian woman, they were held over your head like a sword ever since you hit puberty. It seemed everything you were allowed to do or not allowed to do, could be traced back straight to the damn marriage market. Don't eat all those cakes, you'll put on weight and then nobody will want to marry you. Put on some more weight, Indian men like their women curvy, if you stay so skinny, nobody will want to marry you. Don't stay out too late, don't wear those clothes, don't wear too much make-up, get a whitening facial every week, smile more, wear happier colours, don't be so career-minded, learn how to make round-round chapatis, don't tell anyone your deepest, darkest fears—or nobody will fucking want to marry you. We may as well live in Victorian England. She took a deep breath. Focus, she told herself, focus.

'We were very little, when she told me,' she said, 'she was very scared at the time.'

Laxmi's mother looked distraught. 'Her ... episodes. I remember. At first, we thought it was for attention, you know? Children do that sometimes. Her father ... he'd force her to hold yellow things in her hand. He said it would drive the fear out. She used to scream and scream...' Her eyes brimmed over. 'My poor girl ... she'd scream and cry and clutch on to my saree and beg me to make him stop. But he ... he never listened to me.'

Avantika felt her own eyes moisten, even as her fingers clenched with rage. She forced herself to stay calm. 'Didn't you ... didn't you take her for counselling or something?'

The woman wiped her eyes and gave a strange half-laugh. 'In those days, where was all this counselling and things? And who to ask? If we asked around, people would think that there was something wrong in our daughter's head. And then—'

'...nobody would marry her,' Avantika finished, trying to keep the bitterness out of her voice.

Laxmi's mother looked away. 'Later, when she went to college, we heard of this psychiatrist in Jogeshwari, so we took her to him. He told us it's called xanthophobia. It's not that common, but common enough for them to have a name for it. He gave her some exercises and they had sessions for about a year or so. It helped, a little. But ... all those things when she was a child, it ... it just ... she was never comfortable around yellow things.'

'Did he, did the counsellor say what may have caused this ... xanthophobia? I mean, phobias usually happen because of some traumatic events or something, no?'

A guilty look crept over the woman's face. She said nothing.

'Aunty?' Avantika pressed on, 'It's okay, it's just me—'

The look turned to one of resignation.

'She was very little, two, maybe three, and I, I had taken her to a garden, to play, you know. We were walking among flowers and then I met someone I knew—an old school friend. After ages, you understand? I had just stopped for a chat, when Laxmi ... she wandered away. It couldn't have been more than two minutes, I swear! She hadn't gone very far also, just a few feet away, among a row of flowers, I could see her, she was in my sight. And then, and then, I heard her scream—'

Avantika's throat felt dry. 'What happened?'

Laxmi's mother made a funny little sound, halfway between a sob and a giggle.

'She had gone and touched a flower and there was a big honeybee on it, and it, it stung her!'

'Oh,' Avantika said frowning at the anti-climax. It must've hurt like anything, but that's it? A honeybee?

'Poor child, she cried so much she got a fever. But it wasn't my fault, I swear, it was just two minutes! Who would've thought her entire life would be spoilt by such a small thing!'

Maybe what had actually spoilt her life wasn't so much a bee-sting, but having parents who made a simple phobia seem like the end of the world, Avantika thought. But she kept her thoughts to herself. Aloud she asked, 'What flower was it, any idea?'

Laxmi's mother's brow furrowed as she tried to remember. 'Wait, wait, I know. It was a—'

'Sunflower?'

'You know, I was going to say marigold, but I think you're right.'

I can't be a sunflower, I can't, I can't, I can't!

Avantika clenched her jaw, her ears full of little Laxmi's cries. And then, she looked at the broken woman sitting before her. Her eyes with their faraway look, as if she wasn't really here, but somewhere in a happier past. The grey wisps of hair that once used to be a thick, shiny braid, her daughter's beautiful inheritance. The wrinkled hands, clutched tightly in her lap. And the look of irreversible pain on her face. Suddenly, she couldn't bear to be in this place a minute longer. She stood up.

'I have to go now, Aunty. Please take care of yourself.'

Laxmi's mother followed her to the door. 'Be careful, dear,' she said, pointing to the helmet in Avantika's hand. 'For your mother's sake.'

Avantika nodded and left, filled with a deep sense of melancholy.

Laxmi had gone through all those traumatic experiences and had never breathed a word of it to her. And they had been the best of friends! Perhaps she'd been ashamed? Her parents had certainly made her feel like she had a reason to feel ashamed. If her theory was right, Laxmi hadn't told her even half the story. Maybe she'd wanted to, maybe she just—

'Well, hello there.'

Avantika had been so lost in her thoughts that she hadn't even realized that a man was leaning casually against her scooter. Or that the man was Dhruv.

'What are you doing here?', she demanded.

He gave her a lopsided grin.

'It's a free country, last I checked.'

She folded her hands against her chest and raised her eyebrows.

'Fine, fine,' he said, 'I was at Khotachi Wadi taking a few pictures for that project I'm doing for you guys and I thought I'd swing by and see how Laxmi's folks are doing. I'm guessing that's why you're here?'

She hadn't noticed the smart and clearly very expensive SLR camera case slung on his side. Was he telling the truth, she wondered.

'How come you're suddenly Mr Sympathetic?'

Dhruv looked irritated. 'Right. First, you accuse me of being creepy when all I did was bring you home safely from a bar. Now you're questioning my motives when I want to check on a friend's parents?'

'I thought you said you weren't friends with her.'

'Friends. Acquaintances. Whatever, Sherlock.'

Shifty man, she thought, as she shrugged and pointed to her bike. 'Can I take that or do you have some more leaning on to do?'

He unfolded himself and stepped aside. She got on the bike and put on her helmet. As she was pulling out of the parking space, he smiled.

'You know, I've figured out where we first met.'

'Really.' She sounded sceptical.

'It was at that farewell party, wasn't it? The one Aisha threw right after your tenth standard board exams?'

'Why do you think that?' she asked coldly.

'It was the only time your entire class had come over. I can't forget that point, because Aisha mentioned it at least eight times a day back then.'

She sniffed. 'Yes. Well.'

'What were you, forty? Fifty girls?'

'Forty-five.'

'It was so bloody noisy. I guess that's what happens when girls have fun.'

'Not everyone had fun.'

'No?' He looked genuinely surprised. 'It certainly looked that way.'

She thought of making a snappy response. Don't believe everything you see. That was a good one. Or, maybe, looks can deceive. Naah, too pat. Instead, she snapped her visor down and started the scooter.

'Goodbye,' she said.

He looked a little confused at her abruptness, but smiled anyway. 'See you around.'

She hit the accelerator and zoomed away. Avantika had to get to office and figure out what to do next. If Laxmi's mom was right and Laxmi had suffered from the phobia till recently, then the body couldn't possibly be hers. But then whose was it? And where was Laxmi? And why wasn't anyone else but her asking these questions? She raced past the Worli Naka signal. The road ahead was wide, open and blessedly free of traffic. She revved the scooter—as much as it was possible on a vehicle that started shuddering if you took it beyond 60 kilometres per hour. She opened her visor and felt the cool breeze rush against her face. This is what made riding a bike worth it. The way the air felt against your skin. That feeling of being alone and apart from the crowd, utterly free and as close as you could come to actually flying. Or at least, you know, gliding slowly while faster birds overtook you.

She sighed with pleasure. Up ahead, she saw a dark, wet patch on the road. Probably water spilled from a tanker[1].

---

1 For a metropolitan that calls itself the financial capital of the country, Mumbai and its suburbs routinely face crushing water shortages. It's all a big mystery, considering the city actually has enough reserves to meet 100% of the demand. Perhaps one clue lies in the bellies of water tankers, great big rumbling beasts that leak their way across the city, and make a killing from selling water in places where the water pipelines have spontaneously 'broken.'

She decelerated and gently pressed the brakes. Nothing happened. She pressed the brakes harder. Still nothing. She had a brief moment of panic. But just a moment. Because the next thing she knew, the scooter was sliding on the patch, the handle in her hands feeling as immaterial as air. A sickening sensation as the world came smashing down. A gong in her head as her helmet crashed against the concrete. The faint metallic taste of blood in her mouth.

And then, darkness.

1999

This was a bad, bad idea, Avantika thought, sitting on the edge of the couch. All around her, there was music, laughter, endless chatter. It was the farewell party for the Class of 1999. Venue: Aisha Juneja's palatial bungalow on Napeansea Road. Time: 7 p.m. onwards. On the guest list: Everybody, minus their parents.

There were girls sitting on chairs, comparing notes and outfits. There were girls on the makeshift dance floor, trying to catch the eye of a photographer who was wandering around taking commemorative pictures. There were girls standing shyly in the corner, making eyes at the boys—boys!—among the guests. And then, there was her, sitting alone, wondering what on earth she was doing here. At a party at Aisha's house with forty-four girls who couldn't care less if a giant sea-squid ripped open the dance floor and swallowed her whole mid-Macarena. She wasn't being paranoid. She'd *read* some of the entries in her slam book[2]. So why was she here at all?

But no, that was a silly question. She knew why she was here. It was because Laxmi had accosted her on the last day of the board exams and said, 'Aisha's throwing a party and you should come, because who knows when we'll see each other again?' And she had thought, good point. Some point. So far, she'd seen Laxmi careening from one end of the room to the other, giggling hysterically with Aisha, Mahira and Shweta, and then, talking quietly with a tall, dark-haired boy with strange hair and a face you couldn't take your eyes off.

Aisha's brother, Dhruv. Or so she'd reliably been told by a very giggly Meenal. He was easily the best looking boy in the room, and there were quite a few of those to start with. His friends, presumably, although the easy camaraderie between them and Aisha made her feel that maybe they were her friends too. She sighed and looked at her watch: 8.07 p.m.. She'd been the first one to show up. And as if that wasn't embarrassing enough, she was the most boringly dressed person at the party. She fiddled with the collar of her shirt. It was blue gingham with a zip-up front and it fit her better than all her other tops. And the pants! A smart little navy blue pair, which fit her bottom perfectly and made her feel all ready for college. She'd felt so cool, stepping out in this outfit. But that was before she saw how the others were dressed.

---

2 Like a year book, but girlier. It asked people what their favourite colour was, who their favourite actor was, asked them to write a message for you ... come to think of it, it was actually Facebook, but with glittery stickers.

There were dresses and skirts, some daringly mini, some fashionably flared. There were shorts and rompers and tank tops and most of all, there was make-up. Lips glistened in the yellow lamp-light, cheeks seemed flushed, eyes appeared sultrier than usual and hair was either left loose or styled with shiny hair accessories. There was nobody old enough to raise a disapproving eyebrow at any of it. Even Aisha's parents didn't seem to be chaperoning discreetly from the corner. Perhaps they were around and were staying away to give the kids their privacy? They seemed hi-fi[3] enough to do something like that.

She considered asking someone where the phone was, so she could call Baba and ask him to come pick her up a little earlier. Sure, she had some emergency money, just enough for a taxi back home. But that was a dreadful extravagance. Better to wait till 9.30 p.m.. Baba would come then. Till then, she could have some food, maybe the paneer kebabs she saw floating around on trays held by white-gloved waiters. She was just wondering if she should flag one of them down, when someone sat on the couch next to her. She spun around half-hoping it was Dhruv Juneja, but it was only Laxmi, holding a paper cup in her hands.

'Hi,' she said.

'Hi.'

'I'm glad you came.'

---

3 In pre-globalisation India, anything middle-class morality deemed just a bit much, was automatically 'hi-fi'. Dating someone you didn't mean to marry was hi-fi. Women smoking cigarettes was hi-fi. Gambling on horses was definitely hi-fi. High fidelity audio systems with sweet sound reproduction were … imported.

Avantika gave her a tight smile. She didn't say 'me too'. That would've been lying.

'Thanks for getting her to invite me,' she said instead.

Laxmi looked like she was going to deny it, but then she just shrugged. They both knew that Aisha would never have invited her on her own.

'Can you believe it's over?' Laxmi asked, 'All those ... exams, and studying and that tension? I feel so light.'

'Totally,' Avantika agreed, 'I can sleep at night now, without having nightmares about sitting for a geography exam and being handed an algebra question paper.'

They both laughed and just for a moment there, it was almost exactly like old times. Then Laxmi glanced at the paper cup in her hands and slapped her forehead.

'I forgot only! I came to give you this,' she said, holding out the paper cup, 'have you tried it? It's yummy!'

Avantika took the cup. There was a very light pink liquid inside. 'What is it?' she asked, taking a sip. It tasted sweet and bubbly and happy—like a heartfelt laugh.

'Champagne,' Laxmi said with a grin.

Avantika's eyes widened. She knew about alcohol, of course, she wasn't a total loser. The past couple of years, she'd been allowed to have a small glass of port wine on New Year's Eve. But this was nothing like that. This was ... fancy stuff. This was ... champagne. She took another sip, pretty sure that her parents would disapprove of her drinking among strangers. But all those bubbles were tickling her stomach on the inside and making her feel happy.

'It's ... nice,' she said, grinning.

'Right? Keep the cup, I'll get another.'

And with that, she bounded away. Avantika sat back on the couch, enjoying the warmth that was spreading through her stomach. Through the corner of her eyes, she saw Dhruv talking to some of his friends. She wondered if any of them would ask her to dance. Isn't that how these things went? But no, on second thoughts, they wouldn't. And for some reason, this was not depressing her as much as it normally would've. She pushed her spectacles up her nose and took another sip of the champagne. The photographer passed by with his camera, without a second glance in her direction.

Just then, the music changed. Someone must've told the DJ—there was a DJ!—that Aisha was a Backstreet Boys fan, because he started playing all their best tracks. Stuff you could really move to. He started with *Backstreet's Back* and Avantika's foot started tapping of its own accord. Girls and boys were gravitating to the dance floor now. Then came *We've Got it Goin' On* and she kept the glass down on the floor next to the couch and began moving purposefully towards an empty spot on the dance floor. By the time the DJ put on the new hit single *Larger Than Life,* Avantika was in a world of her own. A world where there was only her, the music and the delicious lightness in her head.

Which is why it took her a couple of minutes to realize that Laxmi had joined her and was dancing right next to her, a fond smile on her face. She gave her a happy grin and continued to dance, not noticing the poisonous look Aisha was throwing at her from across the room. Not noticing when Aisha walked towards her, slowly and silently, a tigress prowling through the grass, and began dancing alongside her. She thought she heard Aisha whisper something in her ears, but the music was too loud for her to hear exactly what she'd said. She only saw, through the pink haze of the champagne, Aisha reach out to her, and in one quick move, pull down the zipper of her shirt.

The music didn't stop but for one terrifying moment, Avantika felt like her heart had. She froze, half in shock, half in shame, as the cool breeze raised goose prickles on her bare skin. She was not wearing her usual cotton slip, because slips were for schoolgirls and she was very soon not going to be one. So, tonight of all nights, she'd chosen to wear nothing but her white cotton training bra underneath. And now, a roomful of strangers—half of them boys—had just seen it.

Through reddening eyes, she fumbled hastily with the zipper, trying to pull it close. Her fingers seemed detached from her body. The zip wouldn't close! She struggled in vain, her eyes blurry with tears. She looked up frantically, hoping nobody had noticed and found herself catching the eye of Dhruv Juneja, who had been about to step on the dance floor. Her eyes widened in horror and his gaze dropped instinctively below her neck. It was just for a second, but it was enough. She gave up trying to wrestle with the stubborn zipper, pulled her shirt close against her chest and stumbling, blinded by tears, ran out of the room. Just as she reached the door, the giggling began.

Outside in the corridor, there was nobody except a few servants, with trays of refreshments. She dodged them and made her way to the restroom she had visited earlier that evening. Thankfully, it was empty. Locking the door behind her, she sank to the floor. Tears streamed slowly down her face, falling on her lap, leaving dark splotches on the gabardine of her pants. The look on Aisha's face. The look on Dhruv's face. The shock on the faces of everyone else, which was already turning to amusement. She closed her eyes, letting the tears flow wordlessly. Moments passed. And then, like a sun rising from behind a raincloud, she felt her anger rise.

How dare she? Her eyes sprang open. What gave her the right? Just because she was rich? Good-looking? She had no *right* to treat anyone like this. Who did she think she was? She wiped her tears with the back of the hand and got to her feet. Her nose was running, so she wiped that too. She looked at her teary-eyed reflection in the bathroom mirror and felt even more furious. With a calmness she didn't really feel, she pulled up the zip of her shirt, right up to her neck. That bitch. That absolute ... c—

There was a tentative knock on the door.

'Avanti? Are you in there?' Laxmi's voice asked from the other side.

Avantika threw open the door and stormed past her.

'I'm really sorry ... about what happened in there—', Laxmi began, hurrying to keep up with her.

Avantika stopped dead in her tracks and turned to face her. '*Sorry?* Please! As if you didn't plan the whole thing with her!'

Laxmi recoiled, as if she'd thrown a snake at her. 'What? Why would you say that?'

'*Why?* You made her invite me! You gave me that champagne—'

'That's unfair! I didn't force you to come! I didn't force you to drink!'

'No,' Avantika said bitterly. 'You didn't. That was my fault. I forgot to be careful around you. I forgot that you're one of them now! That you're *her* friend! Not mine.'

Laxmi stopped walking then. 'We're not ... friends?' she asked softly.

'Not anymore,' Avantika said, her jaw set.

She pushed past her and marched down the corridor towards the main door. Away from the music. Away from the humiliation. Away from the only real friend she'd known in ten years of school.

Thirteen

Uday was at his desk, typing the follow-up piece to the Sion murder. It was a many-headed Ravana of a case. At first, it seemed like a simple crime of passion. Jealous husband, cheating wife, absconding lover. Your garden variety trifecta of neighbourhood gossip. But the more people he talked to, the more complicated it was getting. Apparently, the husband had been married twice before, with one wife dying of a mysterious illness and the other having vanished without a trace. He wondered if the police knew. If they didn't, they'd be told tomorrow morning. By an article with his by-line above it.

He grinned and was considering patting himself on the back, when his phone rang. It was Avantika.

'Yeah?' he asked.

'Hi. Um ... I can' ma'e it to wuh today.'

Uday frowned. 'Why are you sounding like that? No, wait, do I want to know?'

'You 'oo. E's a grea stowy.'

'Can you go somewhere with better network? You're sounding drunk.'

'E's naw the netwuh! Ow. E's ma jaw. I cwashed ma bike.'

Uday sat up instantly. This girl. What was he going to do with her? 'Are you okay?'

'Es. Sotta. Was weahing ma hemmet so…'

'Oh good, then you're not *completely* insane! How the hell did this happen?'

'I donno! Ow. Okay, it huhts to talk.'

Uday drummed at his desk anxiously.

'Are your parents back?'

'Nuh.'

'Do you want me to call them?'

'Nuh! They'll wovvy.'

'Avanti! You need someone to take care of you!'

'Now ya soundin' like ma dad.'

Uday clicked his tongue in frustration. Damned woman didn't know when to turn off the jokes. 'I'm serious! Look, tell me where you are and I'll come and take you to a doctor.'

There was a weird hacking sound, followed by an 'ow'.

'Don' make me laugh. Arready saw the doctuh. Got pills an everythin'. Am home now. Bye.'

The phone clicked and Uday wondered if there was any stone and mortar somewhere among Avantika's ancestors. Because sometimes, talking to her felt exactly like talking to a brick wall.

Avantika looked at herself in the mirror to assess the damage. A cut on the upper lip. A bruised lower jaw that hurt to move. Assorted scratches and cuts on the arms. A tear in her jeans. And her favourite red shirt, ruined. The doctor had put mercurochrome on the cuts making her look, in her opinion, like a bloodthirsty revenant. When she had mentioned this to him, he had cut her off with a scowl.

'Stop complaining about silly things,' he'd growled. 'You're lucky you escaped with nothing broken. You should see some of the bike accidents that I've had to patch up. Youngsters and teenagers who're brought in on stretchers and have to leave on crutches. And sometimes on stretchers.' The scowl had deepened. 'Dead,' he'd added, as if she hadn't realized what 'stretcher' implied.

And with that, he had shooed her out of his office, with dire warnings to take the medication, get some rest and let her body heal itself. Which is what she was doing now, curled up on the sofa in the living room, with a quilt, a mug of cocoa that she sipped through a straw and, most therapeutic of all, a DVD of the BBC adaptation of *Pride and Prejudice* playing on the TV. That Colin Firth. Better than all the muscle relaxants of the world combined. She sighed contentedly and pulled the quilt up to her neck. Soon, she found her eyes drooping of their own accord and with a big yawn, she fell asleep.

She was walking down a long, narrow corridor. It was cold and dark. There were doors on both sides, and one at the very end of the corridor. A slim sliver of blue light escaped from underneath it. This was the door she was walking towards. She could tell that she didn't want to, but it seemed she had no power over her legs, which kept going, left-right, left-right, straight ahead. Goosebumps prickled her flesh and she shuddered. Suddenly, she was aware of shapes in the dark, people standing in the corridor, leaning against the walls. They stared at her with curious, lightless eyes, but let her pass. Just then, one of them grasped her hand. She nearly screamed. It was Shweta.

'Why did you do it?', she hissed. 'Why couldn't you just stay out of it?' She wrenched her hand free and stumbled away from her.

Closer to the door, now. Closer, closer, another step and she'd be able to touch it. She leaned her hand against the door. It opened without protest and she stepped inside. A cavernous room, even colder than the corridor, bathed in dim blue light. Cabinets lined it on three sides, cabinets full of deep drawers that rose high, so high up, all the way to the roof, each with more drawers than you could count. Each drawer had a number on it and, she knew in a way she couldn't explain, a dead body within. The floor was filthy, stained with the reddish-brown crust of dried blood and faeces. Her stomach churned as she stepped over it, but still her legs carried on, left-right, left-right, till suddenly she was in the middle of the vast room.

An operating table stood there, with a figure hunched over it. It seemed to sense her because it raised its head and turned around. Lab coat, face mask, a scalpel dripping blood.

'Oh, you medum,' Ganesh leered holding it out to her, 'Want to do it? She won't mind.'

And then she felt her throat clench with a silent scream—the cadaver he was cutting up, began to rise. Slowly it got up, innards spilling from the incisions in its flesh. Deathly pale and water-bloated, it grinned at her with Laxmi's face. 'Hey, long time no see,' it said and waved. The movement caused ripples in its flesh and just like that, water was pouring out of it in great gushes, taking bits of skin and bone with it.

She wanted to shut her eyes and scream and run away from this place, but she couldn't. The fear had numbed her, rooted her to where she stood, her legs felt weighed down with iron, her tongue heavy as lead. She stood stock-still and shivered, stomach clenched, unable to breathe. And then, a cold hand on her shoulder. She whipped her head around and looked straight into Laxmi's dark eyes. A whole, living Laxmi, not the thing on the table.

'You mustn't believe she is me,' Laxmi told her reproachfully, 'you should know better.'

But as she said this, her face began to blur. Eyes, nose, mouth, all dissolved into one smooth flesh-coloured surface. The faceless Laxmi tilted her head to one side and asked her quizzically, 'What's wrong? Aren't you happy to see me?'

A bell went off then and she saw Ganesh put down the scalpel and move towards her. The cadaver on the table too, got off awkwardly, pushing its intestines back into the gory gash, and began walking towards her. Terror took hold of her then and she raised her hands in front of her face and—

Avantika awoke with a start, gasping for breath. Her heart was hammering in her chest and her breathing was ragged and harsh. Her feet felt icy cold, yet she could feel the sweat on her brow. She gulped hard, hand over heart, waiting for her heartbeat to get back to normal. Then she picked up the quilt that had fallen on the floor and pulled it tightly around herself.

Outside, darkness had fallen and the air was full of the sounds of traffic snarls as thousands of homeward bound commuters got in each other's way. Inside, the TV stood silent, the DVD having run its course without an audience. Avantika blinked a few times. Her head felt fuzzy and every move she made reminded her of all the different places in which her body ached. She got off the couch slowly, to a chorus of sore muscles. Gingerly, she made her way to the kitchen for a glass of water. She had just about poured herself one, when the doorbell rang.

She started a little, still under the spell of the nightmare. Then shaking her head, she opened the door.

'Thank god,' Uday said, 'I was about to call the fire brigade and force this thing open.'

Fourteen

'I've been ringing the doorbell for at least ten minutes now, where were you?' Uday asked, following her into the living room.

'I'd passed out.' Avantika eased on to the sofa, wincing. Everything she did was in slow-motion now, thanks to the pain. 'I think my doctor's given me horse tranquilizers instead of painkillers.'

She moved her lower jaw from side to side experimentally. It hurt, but a lot lesser than it had in the afternoon. Uday glanced at her, his gaze resting a moment on the cut lip and the bruise on her chin.

'You look terrible,' he told her.

'Thanks, you too.'

'Here,' he said, handing her a plastic bag as he sat down on the couch beside her. There was a warm takeaway container inside, with some plastic spoons and tissues. She sniffed at it. He noticed.

'It's chicken soup, not RDX. You said your jaw was hurting so—'

Her stomach must've been listening, because it chose this moment to rumble. She nodded gratefully and took the container out of the bag.

'You are so the man.' She took a gulp straight from the container. Spoons were for the significantly less hungry.

The soup was warm, creamy and delicious, a far cry from the usual restaurant fare of boiled water with sad floating vegetable slivers and the merest hint of chicken stock. She gave a satisfied 'Mmm' and proceeded to finish it with the general enthusiasm of someone auditioning for the lead role in an *Oliver Twist* remake.

'That was so good.' She licked her lips out of habit, then winced. The movement had sent a fresh jolt of pain through her cut lip.

Uday watched her, concerned. 'Feeling better?'

'Lots, yes.'

'Good. Now tell me what happened.'

She told him, leaving out all details of where she was and what she was doing right before the accident. By the time she was done, the look of concern had been replaced with one of puzzlement.

'So ... you're saying ... you were riding your bike, there was a water spill on the road, you lost control of the bike and it skid because your brakes randomly stopped working? That makes no sense.'

'I know.'

'I can understand if it was an oil spill, but water? Nope. Something doesn't fit here.'

'I know.'

'When was the last time you got your bike serviced?'

'Last month? Maybe the month before? It's not been that long.'

'Then there's no obvious reason for your brakes to stop working suddenly.'

'I know. That's why I had a mechanic take a look at them.'

Uday raised his eyebrows, caught between admiration and exasperation. 'How? When did—?'

Avantika shrugged, causing little ripples of pain to flow down her sore back.

'When I was at the doctor. I know the guy, he usually does whatever bike work I need done. I called him and he came and took the keys from me and then he took the bike to his garage.' Then, catching the look of disbelief on his face, she added, 'What? What was I supposed to do? Leave it there?'

'Fair enough,' Uday said, with a grudging shake of his head. 'So what did he say?'

Avantika looked him straight in the eye and with a voice that betrayed no emotion, she replied, 'He said the brake line had been cut.'

Uday's eyes widened. For a moment there was no sound, except the insistent honking of the traffic outside. 'You know what that means.' It wasn't a question.

She nodded.

'Does this have anything to do with what you've been working on?'

'Don't know. It's possible. I don't think I've pissed people off *that* much in my personal life.'

Uday let out a breath. He took in the vivid red splashes of mercurochrome on the cuts on Avantika's hands, the green and purple bruises on her jawline, the angry red cut on her lip.

'Avanti. You've definitely pissed *someone* off. Nobody cuts a brake line for a prank. Do you realize how much worse this could've been? What if there was a truck coming at you when this happened? What if you were speeding on the Western Express Highway and—'

'Don't remind me, okay?' she shot back, annoyed. 'I've already thought about all that. I just ... I don't want to think about it right now. I have enough nightmares as it is.' She shuddered, thinking of the one she'd just woken from.

He leaned towards her and put a hand on her shoulder. She covered her eyes with her hand, taking a deep breath to steady herself. Why was it that she could take anything with her chin up, except a little kindness? She felt her eyes prick and she rubbed them to keep the tears from coming.

'I'm okay,' she said, sniffing and getting up. 'I'll be fine. I just need to ... figure some stuff out.'

Uday stood up and gently caught her arm. 'Let me help,' he said.

She looked into his eyes. He was probably the only one she could trust right now. She nodded.

An hour and a half later, Avantika was exhausted. She had just finished telling Uday everything and it had been like one long, tiring session with a shrink. To his credit, Uday had sat and heard her out patiently, interrupting her just two or three times, and that too, to understand better. Now, he was pacing the room slowly, digesting everything he had heard, while she sat slumped on the couch, idly massaging her aching shoulder and staring at nothing.

'Okay,' he said at last. 'The way I see it, there are a few questions we need answers to. One, where is Laxmi's body? Two, who is this Ajay and what connection, if any, does he have with Laxmi's disappearance, if not her death? And third and most urgent of all, Avanti, who is trying to stop you from finding these things out and why?'

'I actually have a hunch about who Ajay is, but I could be wrong,' she said, rubbing her temples. 'The thing is, every new thing I come across just makes the whole thing more complicated. It's like running in a maze and every day the maze changes, grows bigger or sprouts new byways—'

'Welcome to the plot of "The Maze Runner". Also known as investigative journalism,' said Uday, with a wry smile.

She didn't smile back. 'It's not funny. I don't know how you can still find it funny. Doesn't it sap you, doing this day in, day out? Not knowing the answers, being surrounded by questions that just ...' she waved her hands vaguely, a reporter lost for words. 'How do you keep your head up?'

He gave her a purposely patronising smile. 'Balls of steel, baby,' he said, and then ducked to avoid the cushion she threw at him.

'I'm asking seriously!'

'Seriously? You think about the outcome. Keep your mind on the good you're trying to do. And hope like hell that it works.'

'That's not what you said the last time I asked. That time you said it's something about starfish.'

'Oh, yeah, heh,' he said, looking away shiftily, 'forget about that. It's this, the outcome thing.'

'Shut up and tell me the starfish story.'

'How can I shut up and then—?'

'Just tell me!'

He made a face. 'Fine. It's this story I'd read. I think it's a good analogy for what we do. You know, working despite the odds in a country where—'

'Story!'

'Fine, fine! So this old man was walking down a beach, where lots of starfish had washed up, right? Then he sees this girl, this little girl, chucking them back into the sea, one by one. The old man says to her, "Why're you doing this? There are thousands of them out here. You'll never be able to save them all." The girl looks at him calmly. Then she bends down, picks up a starfish, throws it into the sea and says, "I saved *that* one, didn't I?"'

Avantika smiled despite herself. So sappy. So utterly well-meaning and good and idealistic. You couldn't help liking someone who thought like this. She had the weirdest urge to reach out and pull Uday's cheeks. Uday himself, clearly felt like he had embarrassed himself no end, because he looked away and cleared his throat.

'So. Yeah. Basically that. Mention this to anyone else and I'll kill you.'

'Oh please. Get in line.'

Uday laughed. Then, some part of his brain must have nudged him because he suddenly stopped laughing and sat up straight. 'Wait, what do you mean you have a hunch who Ajay is?'

Avantika shrugged. 'It's a guess. There is *some* proof to support it, but nothing concrete.'

'Fuck that, who is this guy?'

'Well, for starters ...' she began, but was cut short by the doorbell.

Uday looked at his watch. 10.26 p.m. 'Were you expecting someone?', he asked.

She shook her head quizzically and walked to the door. She peered through the spy hole. Then, slowly, with a wary look on her face, she backed away.

'What?' Uday asked, 'Who is it?'

'Dhruv,' she said, frowning.

'Juneja? At this time? Why?' Uday demanded.

'I don't know ... but ... oh God—' Avantika bit her lip. Her throat suddenly felt dry.

'What?' Uday asked. He was on his feet now.

'He ... he was the last person I met before I ... before the accident.'

The doorbell rang again.

'Okay...' Uday said, unsure of where this was going. Or indeed, of what it implied.

'I came out from Laxmi's building and he was ... he was leaning against my bike. As if ... as if he was waiting for me.'

She looked at him, and for the first time, he saw a flash of fear in her eyes. He realized what she was trying to say.

The doorbell rang again.

Fifteen

Avantika stared at the door, thinking fast. Dhruv coming to her house, could mean many things. If he was the one who'd sabotaged her Activa, maybe he was coming over to make sure that she was good and done with. Or, a dark corner of her mind prodded, to finish the job. No, wait, that was ridiculous. This was a very well-to-do, respectable man who was a part of her social circle. If he wanted to kill her, why would he get his own hands messy? Especially, in a city like Mumbai where people were so desperate for money, they could bump someone off for the price of an unlimited rice plate[1].

'I'm opening the door,' she told Uday. She had never felt this glad to have him around.

---

1 A rice plate is the original value meal, designed to fill the appetites* of working men who hadn't yet acquired wives or had left the ones they'd acquired back home in the village. What it lacks in quality, it makes up for in unlimited quantities of rice, roti, dal, sabzi and if the rice plate house is particularly posh, a chunk of roasted papad.

* Well, at least the stomach-related ones.

Taking a deep breath, she opened the door. If there was any doubt in her mind that Dhruv had something to do with her accident, it was confirmed by the look on his face. But, and this was where the confusion set in, as guilty as he looked, he seemed more horrified. She knew what a horrified man looked like. She'd seen her father's face, whenever she'd shown him her maths test results.

'Hey! Wassup?' she said in a cheery voice, while her face refused to keep up with the act.

Dhruv shook his head, as if he couldn't believe what he was seeing.

'Fuck,' he said and ran his hand through his hair.

'You say the sweetest things.'

He clasped his hands together tightly, his face very serious.

'I need to talk to you ...,' he began, just as Uday came and stood behind Avantika, blank-faced and mildly menacing.

A quick flash of recognition.

'... alone,' he finished.

Avantika shook her head. 'N-ooo, I'm still getting over what happened after the last time we talked alone.'

Dhruv blinked. He looked from Avantika to Uday, the accusation sinking in. 'Hold on—you think ... you don't think *I* had anything to do with this?'

They just glared at him. Avantika crossed her arms across her chest. Dhruv, was blinking furiously, his clasped fingers twitching, all his usual suavity missing in action.

'It's not what you think,' he said. 'I swear. You have to trust me.'

Avantika remembered the road rushing towards her, the sickening crank of the fenders grazing the concrete, the taste of blood in her mouth.

'Do I?' she whispered, and then turning her head slightly in Uday's direction she asked, 'Do I have to trust him?'

Not taking his eyes off Dhruv, he shook his head. Dhruv looked away from him and turned to Avantika.

'You know you can trust me,' he said, in a quiet voice. 'If I wanted to harm you, I could've done it when you were sleeping at my place.'

Uday blinked at this. 'What!' he said, forgetting his menacing henchman act for a second. 'When did this happen?'

Avantika closed her eyes in exasperation. Boys. They had no sense of priorities sometimes.

'A while ago,' she said. 'It's not what you think.'

'That's what I'm saying,' Dhruv muttered.

She pointed a threatening finger at him. 'It's not the same thing,' she growled. 'I could've died! Do you understand that?'

'I do, I do, but—'

'And you still expect me to hear you out? You're insane!'

'I don't want you to hear me out,' Dhruv said in a resigned voice, 'I ... want you to come with me.'

Avantika looked at him as if he had suggested she turn into a rabbit for some time. Then she gave a hollow, humourless laugh and walked into the living room, shaking her head. Dhruv made as if to follow her, but Uday moved forward, blocking his entry. The two men eyeballed each other for a moment, then Dhruv gave an exasperated sigh and stepped back. He seemed to reach a decision.

'I know you want to know what happened to Laxmi,' he called out to Avantika, who was in the process of slowly sitting down on the couch.

She didn't look at him, but the way she stared straight ahead, told him she was listening.

'I can help, but you have to come with me,' he said. 'I promise you, you're not in danger.' And then, remembering the events of the afternoon, he added awkwardly, 'anymore.'

All he got was two sullen stares. He held up his hands in a conciliatory way. 'Tell you what, I'll wait downstairs in my car for half an hour. You think it over and if you think you can trust me, please come down.'

And with that, he was gone.

Uday shut the door behind him and walked over to the couch. 'You want to order dinner?' he asked, sitting next to her on the couch and scrolling through his phone for a food app. 'I'm starving. And that soup couldn't have been enough for you.'

He waited for a response, but Avantika was still staring straight ahead, lost in thought. 'Avanti?'

'Mmm?'

'Dinner?'

'No. I think … I'll go with him.'

Uday hit the couch in frustration. 'Are you out of your bloody mind? This guy could be the one who tried to kill you and you want to go with him god knows where in the middle of the fucking night? You're fucking suicidal or what?'

Avantika covered her face with her palms and slowly rubbed her eyes.

'No,' she said slowly, 'I'm just sick of it all. I've had an old friend turn up dead, found out things about her and her parents that I was better off not knowing, met and talked to people I really, really didn't want to and been thrown off my bike so half my body aches like a motherfucker. I'm in pain, I'm mindfucked and I'm just ... so ... *sick* ... of it all!'

Uday reached out to put an arm around her, but she shrugged it off.

'And the worst part, Uday, is that I still don't have any answers! All I have is a theory and that's ... a little out there. This not knowing anything for sure, it's driving me insane!'

'That doesn't mean you just—'

'What, go with a guy who claims to have the answers? Isn't that what you would've done?'

'That's different... '

'Why?'

She was looking at him now, challenging him to answer. She knew what he was going to say. That the worst thing that could've happened to him if he did something like this, was that he'd be found dead somewhere. The worst thing that could happen to her, was that she'd be found alive and raped, in a state that was worse than death. It was what anyone would've said. But Uday didn't. He just looked at her, shook his head sadly and looked away.

'At least don't go alone, let me come—'

'You *know* that won't work.'

'No, I don't. At least let's give it a shot?'

'Dhruv won't—'

'He doesn't make the rules—'

'Uday. No.'

He glared at her for a second, then with an exasperated huff, he got up and reached into his pocket. 'Take this then,' he pushed a Swiss Army knife in her hands. 'At least it'll give you *some* chance if things go wrong.'

She pulled open a blade experimentally, just as he warned: 'Careful, it's sharp.'

She pushed the blade back in and went to her bedroom to change.

Dhruv looked at his watch. It was almost 11.30 p.m. Another couple of minutes and he'd have to leave, knowing exactly what Avantika thought of him and how terribly wrong she was. He sighed. There was nothing else to it. You couldn't convince someone of your innocence if they were determined to think of you as guilty. He'd really hoped she'd come and he'd get a chance to redeem himself. He liked her, her sharp mouth and blunt ways. He was about to turn the key in the ignition when he saw her walking towards his BMW, Uday by her side.

Avantika had changed from the long, faded nightshirt she'd worn, into a t-shirt and jeans. She carried a small rucksack with what she called her survival kit—some rope, a small bottle of water, a napkin, a wireless phone charger. Instead of her usual ballet flats, she wore running shoes; partly because they were comfortable and partly because it always pissed her off when stupid women in horror movies wore heels to go away for a weekend to an isolated cottage. They might as well paint a large target sign on their skimpy tank tops with 'Stab Here' written in neon paint right under it.

As Dhruv held open the door to the passenger seat, Uday held her back for a moment. Then he pointedly opened the door to the seat behind the driver's. The two men looked at each other for a second, then Dhruv gave a quick nod, closed the door and went and sat in the driver's seat.

Uday turned to Avantika. He'd appealed to her one last time before they left her apartment. 'Think of your parents,' he'd pleaded. 'If something happens to you—'

And she'd thought of the shell of a woman that Laxmi's mother had turned into and had nearly changed her mind. But then, she'd thought of her own mother. Aai had taught her to finish what she started. She'd be terrified if she knew what Avantika was up to. But she'd never want her daughter to walk away from a situation just because things had gotten a little ... difficult.

And in the end, that's what had made her decide to go. Now, as she eyed the seat behind Dhruv, her stomach tightened with worry. She grit her teeth and gulped. It's okay, she told herself. My phone's location services are on. And I have that emergency app for women. One click of a button and Uday will get an SOS with my exact coordinates. How long it would take him to reach her after that, who knew.

Now, as she was about to enter the car, Uday gave her a quick one-armed hug. 'Call, okay?,' he said. 'Or at least text.'

She nodded and fastened the seatbelt. Uday walked to the front of the car and with a meaningful glare at Dhruv, took a picture of the car, with its number-plate. Then he stepped back. The key turned in the ignition and a couple of moments later, the BMW pulled out of the building's parking lot and zoomed down the empty road outside.

Sixteen

The street lamps shone orange through the windows of the car, falling behind rapidly in quick succession, as the car gained speed. Dhruv was a good driver and he'd got them on to the Western Express Highway remarkably quickly, given the traffic on the roads. That was the thing about Mumbai. The city never slept. There were always people going to work, people coming home from work, people with no work trying to find work and the Civil Works Department giving people work by digging up city roads with a gleeful disregard to public convenience. There was always something going on. Even at 11.15 at night.

They took a right and entered the traffic snarl otherwise known as the Jogeshwari–Vikhroli Link Road. Cars were predictably lined up bumper to bumper, their tail lights like so many angry red eyes glaring at those foolish enough to look at them. Avantika looked away uneasily and glanced at Dhruv through the rear-view mirror.

He was looking straight ahead, presumably focusing on the traffic. Neither of them had spoken a word since leaving Avantika's home. Her own mind, on the other hand, was a chaos of voices. Are you out of your mind, one asked. Relax, you're doing the right thing, another one piped up. And when has *that* ended up well for you, asked the first one. She ignored them. But the silence in the car was making it difficult to drown them out altogether. In any case, she was in it now. There was no going back. Oh please, said a weary little voice within her, it's a stalled car, just open the damn door and run for it. She cleared her throat.

'So ... where are we going?'

Dhruv started a bit, as if he hadn't expected her to speak at all. But he quickly recovered and replied, 'You'll find out.'

Avantika rolled her eyes. 'Are you going to blindfold me now, so I don't know the way to your lair?'

He almost smiled. 'You've already seen my lair. You've spent a night there, remember?'

'Look, can you just ... please ... not put it like that. It makes it seem like I ...,' she fished around for the right word and settled for, 'makes it seem shady.'

'You know what I mean.'

'Yes, I just wish you said what you *actually* mean.'

He didn't reply. She looked out of the window, read five number plates for want of anything better to do, then gave up. 'How did you know about the bike crash?' she asked.

'Shibani,' he replied. 'Your ... friend ... must've told her. She told me, when I went to the office. Right after she asked me if I could get her a complimentary purse from Aisha's new collection.' He shook his head in amusement. 'She's a real character,' he added.

Avantika considered this a blatant understatement. 'Yes, she is. And Uday is not a significant pause kind of friend.'

Why she was explaining this to Dhruv was beyond her, but it seemed important to make that clear, for some reason. He simply shrugged in reply. The signal turned green and the cars and rickshaws around them started moving. They didn't speak for some time, as Dhruv manoeuvred the car through the dense traffic, made up largely of people who had heard of lane discipline and dismissed it as a silly rumour.

At the T-junction at the end of the road, Dhruv took a left turn and alarm bells began ringing in Avantika's head.

'Hold on,' she said, 'doesn't this road go to New Bombay[1]?'

'And to Thane, Panvel, Pune. It depends on where you want to go really.'

'Where *do* we want to go?'

'You'll see.'

'You're trying my patience,' she said slowly and in the rear view mirror she saw the jaunty smile slide off his face.

'Sorry,' he muttered, 'it's just ... we'll be there soon.' And seeing the expression on her face he added, 'There's nothing to be scared of.'

She pulled herself up at this. 'I'm not scared,' she lied. 'I just want to get to the bottom of this bloody affair as soon as possible, that's all.'

She looked away and stared out of the window. The flyovers of New Bombay were glowing orange under the streetlights and there weren't many cars on the road. Dhruv

---

1 A distant suburb of Mumbai, newer than Bombay, but not very Bombay really. Natives and civil servants refer to it as Navi Mumbai. South Bombay residents or 'townies' don't refer to it at all.

stepped on the accelerator and they shot ahead, leaving behind wide, half empty roads, stately office buildings and tree-lined avenues. The BMW had beautiful suspension and the smooth gliding motion of the car made Avantika's eyelids droop. And then, shut.

'We're here.'

Dhruv's voice made her eyes fly open and she woke up with a start, breathing heavily, her heart racing. I have got to stop waking up like this, she thought. How did I sleep in the first place? Must've been the damned painkillers. How strong *were* those things? She felt groggy as hell.

'Are you okay? Relax, relax,' Dhruv was saying.

She nodded and rubbed her face with both hands. He got out of the car and held the door open for her. She stepped out with her backpack and shivered without meaning to. They were parked in a neat, well-maintained driveway. A large bungalow loomed in the darkness before them. All the lights were out. Behind it, far away, Avantika could see the glittering lights of the Mumbai–Pune Expressway. So. Lonavala, then. Or Khandala. That's where they were. In one of the twin hill stations between Mumbai and Pune. There was no way of knowing exactly where. There was no way of knowing where to run.

The night was cool enough to raise goosebumps on her bare skin. She rubbed her arms vigorously, wishing she'd carried a sweater along. When you're cold, you feel more scared, because the physical reactions to fear and mild hypothermia are the same and that confuses the body. Now, where had she read that? And could there be a more irrelevant time to remember this? Blowing warm air on her rapidly freezing palms, she turned to Dhruv, who was fishing out a bunch of keys from his pocket.

'This way,' he said, indicating the bungalow.

Avantika took a long look at it. It seemed a little uncharitable to call it just a bungalow. It was actually a well-proportioned, well-maintained two-storeyed villa done in red brick, with black iron grills and a neat lawn. It would've looked suitably olde worlde and grand in the daylight. In the darkness of night, it looked like a place where prostitutes went to die.

She shuddered and followed Dhruv as he walked up the steps to the main door. It was quiet, aside from the chittering of crickets. He unlocked the door, but it refused to budge. A hard push. A door chain jangled on the other side of the door. He gave a frustrated sigh and rang the doorbell. The sound shattered the silence like a gunshot. A couple of minutes passed. He rang the bell again. This time, a small light came on in a window upstairs. A minute later, the light above the doorway was switched on, just as the ground floor lights came on. Avantika held her breath. She hoped, prayed that her theory was correct. Otherwise, she was walking into ... she had no idea what came after that.

The door opened.

Aisha stood in the doorway. She was wearing a chunky navy blue sweater over boxers printed with poodles. She looked confused and sleepy in equal parts. Then she noticed Avantika standing behind Dhruv and a look of complete exasperation passed her face.

'For fuck's sake!' she hissed at Dhruv.

Avantika found herself breathing again.

'Nice seeing you too,' she muttered.

'Come on in,' Dhruv said to her, ignoring his sister. He took a step forward.

'No!' Aisha said, standing her ground. She held a warning finger in front of Dhruv. 'Not her.'

Dhruv looked at her calmly, but Avantika could sense his anger. 'Let us in. You're in enough trouble as it is. I know about Manek.'

'What about him?'

Aisha had folded her arms across her chest. Her face was poker-player blank. Dhruv didn't reply, but his glare was intimidating enough to make Aisha look away. He pushed her out of the way lightly and entered the house, with Avantika following close behind.

Most of the ground floor was taken up by the large living room with a spiral staircase on one side leading to the floor above. A handsome green Chesterfield sofa stood in the centre of the room and it was on this that Dhruv parked himself. Avantika chose to sit on one of the plush leather chairs next to the sofa. Aisha stood by the door for a few seconds, looking helpless and angry at the same time. Then she shut the door with an exasperated huff and came and sat down on an incongruous fainting couch that stood on the other side of the sofa.

'Look, I can explain—' she began, but Dhruv held up a hand and she stopped.

'Do you remember what I'd told you the day we found out about him?'

Aisha didn't reply, but her gaze fell to her lap, where her fingers were fidgeting. Avantika had never seen her looking so unsure before.

'Aisha…?' Dhruv asked. There was a sharp big-brother edge to his voice.

'I remember, I remember, okay? You told me never to call him for anything.'

'For *anything*,' Dhruv said. 'You had promised. Do you remember promising me that?'

There was a mumbled 'yes'.

'But you called him anyway.'

'I'm sorry,' Aisha said slowly. 'I didn't think—'

'No, you didn't.' In one brisk movement, Dhruv got up and strode to her angrily. 'You never do. You've always been pretty thoughtless, but this is too much! Even for you!'

He pointed to Avantika. 'She could've lost a limb, died,' he said through gritted teeth. 'You would've been thrown in jail for it. Did you stop to think about *that* before you picked up the phone and called a man who kills people for money?'

Seventeen

Avantika blinked. A cold, dark abyss was opening in the pit of her stomach. The bike. The accident. It was Aisha. She could feel her heart thudding in her chest.

'You … what?'

'It was a misunderstanding,' Aisha said, not meeting her eyes.

Avantika tried to think of a response for this. The road flashed before her eyes, the concrete rising to meet her. She remembered the heat from the friction of flesh and asphalt, scraping her arms raw. Her fingers twitched.

'A misunderstanding,' she said, anger making her voice shake. 'What had you sent him to do? Origami?'

Aisha rolled her eyes and in that instant, Avantika felt like gouging her eyes out. Her fingers clenched into fists.

'Am I boring you? Sorry. I'll just sit here and shut up and let you tell me how this tiny little misunderstanding happened, this small fucking mistake that could've oh, I don't know, maybe FUCKING KILLED ME A BIT!'

She had gotten to her feet without realizing it. Aisha, on the other hand, was sitting sullenly on the couch, not looking in her direction. No apology, no justification. Not that it would have helped, but this total indifference infuriated Avantika. It must've shown on her face, because Dhruv sounded sincerely apologetic when he said, 'You deserve an explanation, Avantika. Will you sit down please, so I can give you one?'

She spun around and looked him right in the eyes. He flinched at the look on her face. Then he held up his hands.

'Please?'

She sat down, anger bubbling inside her like hot poison. Her whole body felt tense, like a taut bowstring. She didn't want to listen to whatever this man had to say. But there was a miserable look on his face, which was urging her to hear him out. She could sense real regret there. So she took a deep breath, bottled up the boiling venom for now and gave him a curt nod. He nodded back gratefully.

'Our father,' he began and faltered for a moment before resuming. 'He was very ... successful in his professional life. We had everything we ever wanted, books, toys, bikes, you name it. Ma was a part of all kinds of charitable societies, and between her fellow members and Dad's friends and clients, we had a lot of people coming home in those days.'

He sat down on the couch next to Aisha, who was still looking at her hands, not saying anything. 'One of them was a man we were told to call Manek Uncle. A very quiet man. Always in a safari suit. Neat side-parted hair. He'd bring us chocolates, Cadbury's Eclairs.'

'Dhruv, don't. Please,' Aisha muttered without looking up.

He ignored her and stared straight ahead, a faraway look in his eyes.

'Then, one day, I came home from college and Ma and Dad were having a huge fight. They didn't fight all that much usually—maybe they did it when we weren't around. Anyway, I'd never heard them fight like that, so loudly, so after a while I went to check. Dad stopped yelling when I entered the room, but Ma lost it completely. "Tell him," she said. "Tell your son what his father has been up to, how he has made his money." Then she started flinging things on the floor, flower-pots, books, photo frames, anything she could get her hands on. She had this look on her face, as if just looking at all those things was disgusting for her. I thought she had gone mad. I tried to stop her, but she just kept screaming "Tell him, tell him" at my dad and then she broke down crying.'

He let out a pained sigh as if the memory was a physical object, wrenching his insides. 'By that time, Aisha had also come back from college. So Dad sat us down and told us. About our nice Manek Uncle and how Dad had been paying him for years, to make ... inconvenient people ... disappear.' Dhruv's voice sounded dead now. 'He said that Ma didn't understand, that sometimes there is no other way left. Sometimes, for you to stay safe and sound, someone else had to ... go.'

He pinched the bridge of his nose. 'They separated a couple of months after that, Ma and Dad. She couldn't bear the idea of being with a man who had actually killed people. But before he left, Dad took Aisha and me aside and gave us Manek's number. He said he had business rivals, who were even more ruthless than he was. People who could perhaps harm us one day, to get to him. I don't know if he was just being paranoid and I never asked. He was run over by a car a few months after the separation.'

For a moment, nobody spoke. Aisha had not looked up since Dhruv started talking. Dhruv himself was still gazing into the distance, as if seeing something the others couldn't. Avantika sat frozen, her mind reeling. She couldn't remember if she'd ever seen Aisha's father. There was a fleeting memory of her mother—a tall, graceful woman, soft-spoken and elegant in her chiffons and silks. To discover this horror hidden underneath the facade of upper class respectability ... She shook her head. The movement seemed to snap Dhruv out of his reverie.

'That day when you ran into me outside Laxmi's house, it wasn't by accident.'

Avantika nodded. 'I figured.'

'I wasn't lying though, I was actually in the neighbourhood taking pictures. But, then I saw someone who looked exactly like Manek crossing the road. He was heading into Laxmi's lane and I don't know why, but I got suspicious. I followed him and when I got close, I saw that it *was* Manek. Same side parting, same safari suit. He was older than I remembered, naturally, but it was definitely him. There was a row of bikes parked outside Laxmi's building and he was crouched near one of them. When I called out to him, he stood up. I introduced myself and chatted a bit about old times, not letting on that I knew what he really did for a living. He told me he had dropped his keys and had just found them when I called out to him. Damned casual. There was nothing suspicious about him at all. Still, I felt like something was off, so I waited a bit after he left. And then ... you showed up.'

'And you didn't say *a word* about it.'

'What could I've said? All I knew was that he was near your bike for a few minutes. I only guessed what he must've been doing there, after Shibani told me you'd had an accident.'

He looked spent now, and there was a pleading air about him as if he was asking for absolution. Avantika ignored him and turned to Aisha, who was sitting motionless next to him. 'Your turn,' Avantika told her.

Aisha gave her an insolent stare. 'For what?'

'Don't play games. Why did you send that man to kill me? *Kill* me, Aisha, God, what was I doing that was so—'

She broke off, staring at the woman. 'Oh,' she said, 'You didn't ... oh.'

Then she laughed. Dhruv and Aisha exchanged a bewildered look.

'You know,' Avantika looked amused, till you saw her eyes. 'You think you're really shrewd and cunning and stuff, but God, Aisha, you're just like the rest of us.' Her expression turned bitter. 'When you're scared, you panic and do the kind of stupid shit no sane person would ever do.'

Aisha frowned. 'What are you talking about?'

'You must've been scared shitless, na. And I think I know why. Should I spell it out?'

She didn't wait for an answer. 'You heard I was asking questions about Laxmi, meeting her mom, stalking Shweta, meeting Mahira and you freaked out. Because you were scared I'd find out things. Things like Laxmi was dating someone, someone her dad didn't approve of. Or that the body in the morgue which you so conveniently turned to ashes, wasn't Laxmi's in the first place. How could it be? It was wearing a yellow t-shirt and Laxmi, well, she was terrified of yellow, wasn't she?'

Avantika paused to smile at the gasp. 'Yes, I knew. And I know *you* know. Blue sunflowers on a handbag, huh? So sweet of you.'

She watched Aisha's face closely, which was getting paler by the second.

'The thing is, though, why would me knowing these things freak you out to the extent of hiring a hit-man? I mean, the automatic suspect is usually the missing boyfriend, right? But then again, why would a friend, even a best friend, *never* have a yellow bag in her collection, just because her friend doesn't like that colour? Seems a bit much, doing this kind of a thing for a friend. But for a ... girlfriend? Hmmm,' she tapped the side of her face with a finger, in a mock-thoughtful way. 'How romantic is that, Aisha? Or, do you prefer to be called something else ... *A.J.*?'

You had to give her credit, Avantika thought. Even while someone was tearing down her house of cards, Aisha's face didn't betray any uncertainty. She wondered if she could just reach out and slap some into it.

'I told you she's clever,' said a voice from the other end of the room.

Avantika turned in her seat. A woman was standing at the top of the staircase, wearing a Dora the Explorer nightshirt. Her hair was cut short like Uma Thurman from *Pulp Fiction* and the ends of it were a rich plum colour. She wore a silver nose-ring and a good-natured smile. Her face was vaguely familiar, but the voice Avantika recognized in an instant.

'Hi,' Laxmi said. 'Long time no see!'

Eighteen

Yawning widely, Laxmi walked down the staircase and into the living room. The haircut wasn't the only thing different about her. Her face, once skinny and happy, was now fuller. Her eyes still shone with mischief, but there was a brittle quality to it. Avantika got up from the sofa, walked up to her and suddenly felt horribly awkward.

What did you do when you met someone who used to be your best friend, but whom you've not seen hide or hair of, for the past seventeen years? Worse, what did you do if you'd discovered a minute ago that she wasn't dead as suspected, but alive, well, and had a pretty bizarre taste in nightwear? Somehow, a hug seemed out of the question. And a handshake, well, it's hardly as if they were at the Geneva Convention. Avantika decided to go with a tentative smile, but her stomach beat her to it.

It growled.

Laxmi raised her eyebrows. Avantika grimaced.

'Sorry, I didn't really have a proper dinner so—'

'No, of course, how rude of us!' said Laxmi. 'Let me see if there's something to eat.'

She bounded to the kitchen and opened the large, double-door refrigerator.

Ten minutes later, Avantika was wolfing down a strawberry jam-and-butter sandwich. This is the part where I wake up, she thought, now would be a good time for that.

Here she was, in the middle of Lonavala, or possibly Khandala, eating a sandwich made by an allegedly dead woman, sitting on a couch across a girl who had paid someone to have her killed, and a stone's throw away from a man who had known about everything, but had decided it wasn't worth mentioning. If the Grim Reaper popped up right now and offered her a free margarita, she wouldn't be the least bit surprised.

She stole a look at Laxmi and Aisha, who were sitting side by side on the fainting couch, their hands entwined. The whole thing seemed a bit unreal, to be honest.

'Death suits you,' she said, trying not to stare.

Laxmi gave her a wry smile. 'There's being dead and there's ... being *dead*.'

'Ah, and which one were you hoping I'd be, A.J?' asked Avantika.

Aisha clucked her tongue in irritation. 'Look! ... God! It wasn't like that, okay? I'd asked Manek to stop you, not bloody kill you. How did I know he'd confuse "stop" with "kill"?'

Avantika could not believe how the woman was still refusing to take responsibility for her actions.

'Yes, you'd think hired killers understood the subtle nuances between stopping someone and stopping someone forever. Murderers these days, I tell you,' she said.

Laxmi gave her a strained smile. 'She's telling the truth, you know. I know it doesn't seem that way to you, but there are some things she's just not capable of.'

And Avantika thought of a teacher who'd lost her job for not giving a role in a school play to the right girl. 'Empathy, for one,' she muttered.

Aisha shot her a dirty look, but Laxmi laughed.

'Oh God,' she said, shaking her head, 'You've never really gotten over that whole peeing in class thing, have you?' She held up a hand, as Avantika opened her mouth to protest. 'I'm kidding, I'm kidding. Look, we're all grown-ups here. Can't you just ... forget about what happened and we can just ... carry on?'

Avantika stared at her in disbelief. 'Forget it? I could've died!'

'But you didn't!' Laxmi said, holding up her hands cheerily, 'Let Aisha apologize properly and let's just ... move on, na.'

Avantika shook her head slowly, refusing to believe what she was hearing. Who was this woman? She was nothing like the girl she remembered from school. She brought her palms together, in a gesture of supplication.

'This isn't school, I haven't had my eraser stolen! A "sorry" won't be enough. How can you be so blasé about this? What about your parents? Your dad? Did you know he's gone into shock? He can't talk anymore? And your mum, she's—'

She didn't get to finish the sentence, because Laxmi finished it for her.

'Let me guess, crying a lot?' she said, with the cheery smile intact on her face. The effect was chilling. Avantika found herself speechless.

'She's good at that, you know, my mother,' Laxmi continued, a bitter note entering her voice, 'Crying, wringing her hands, making people feel sorry for her. As if any of that helps.'

'But ... but Laxmi ... your mom ... she's ... how can you—?'

This time it was Aisha who didn't let her complete the sentence. 'You don't know anything, okay?' she said, pointing an angry finger at her. 'You don't get to judge her, you don't get to walk in here and act like you know everything and—'

'Shut up,' Avantika shot back. 'Didn't your dad teach you to speak only when spoken to? Or was it just assassination tips?'

Aisha started as if she had been slapped and even Dhruv looked aghast.

'Hey, watch it!' he said, 'You don't talk about people's parents like that.'

'No? How about your asshole sister? Can I talk about her like that?'

Aisha sprang to her feet. 'Enough!' she hissed. Turning to Dhruv she said, 'Get her out of here *right* now! What the fuck were you thinking, bringing her here? She's a fucking reporter, Dhruv! You want to fuck her, that's your business, but don't rat me out to get into her pants!'

Dhruv stood up, his expression stormy. When he spoke, his voice was quiet with menace.

'Sit. Down.'

Aisha stood her ground, glaring at him.

'Guys...,' Laxmi began, 'let's all calm down—'

They both ignored her.

'Just because you're my sister doesn't mean you can say whatever the fuck you want to!' Dhruv's voice was rising.

'What you have done, what you almost did, could've ruined us! As a family. Do you understand that? Can your tiny mind realize the magnitude of that? I didn't bring her here to rat you out. I brought her here so you could beg her, *beg* her to not go to the police—'

'She had no proof to go to the police with! *Now*, she can, thanks to you!'

Avantika was watching Laxmi, as the argument raged. Aside from the first feeble attempt to mediate, she had been silent. Now, as she caught Avantika's gaze, she nodded vaguely in the direction of the kitchen and headed there. Avantika followed quietly. Behind them, the argument was gaining volume.

Laxmi was suppressing a yawn, as she heaped spoons full of instant coffee into two mugs. 'Brothers and sisters, huh?,' she said, pouring water into an electric kettle. 'Makes you glad to be an only child. Milk?'

Avantika nodded. Laxmi opened the fridge and brought out a tetrapack of milk. She poured some into each mug.

'How can you be so ... so calm right now?'

'Oh, I've seen them fight before. They'll get over it. Sugar?'

'One spoon. No ... I meant, how can you be so calm about ... this whole thing?'

Laxmi handed her the mug of coffee. Avantika took it, warming her hands on the hot stoneware.

'How can you ... how can you let your parents think you're dead?' She ran her fingers through her hair. 'I spoke to your mom, I know how bad things were for you, growing up. And okay, I'm sure your dad wasn't crazy about you being gay, but ... I mean ... couldn't you guys talk it out with him? To ... to punish them like this ... this is your mom's worst nightmare, Laxmi. And your dad ... he must've felt ... God, the man can't talk anymore! He's obviously been hit by this.'

Laxmi took a sip of her coffee and gave a sigh of pleasure. 'I don't know why he was so surprised,' she said, 'it's what he wanted, after all.'

LAXMI SWAMINATHAN

1983–~~2018~~

The first thing she remembered learning was how to keep a secret. Don't tell anyone, don't mention it, don't even think of it, Amma and Appa would say. And she'd nod quietly, dark eyes serious, as if she understood this. She didn't. She couldn't. How do you not think of something that terrified you? Trying not to think of it, meant thinking about not thinking about it. Didn't they realize that? But she tried. Obedience, like brushing her teeth before bedtime, was a good habit they had ingrained into her early in life.

She looked away, heart thudding like a cement crusher when someone in school passed by with a bright yellow water bottle. She practised not wincing when someone wore a buttercup-print dress on their birthday. She politely refused, nails digging deep into the soft flesh of her palms, when someone offered her a lemon-flavoured candy, sweet and tart, shaped liked a lemon wedge and so very visible through the transparent plastic wrapping. And while every encounter with that horrible colour had her screaming herself hoarse on the inside, on the outside she was calm and composed, a normal young woman, without any silly fears that could make her family feel ashamed of her.

But this is the thing about keeping secrets: there's only room for one, if the one you're keeping is big enough. And as the years passed, she came to realize, to her horror, that she had another secret to keep. And this one, was gigantic.

She liked girls. Not in the way she liked, say books, or Boyzone songs, or Cadbury's Crackle. She liked-liked girls. Everywhere around her, they were talking about how cute Salman Khan looked in HAHK, but she'd only had eyes for Madhuri Dixit with her sparkling smile and her flirty coyness. From the first moment the actress had come on screen, she had felt a curious flutter in her chest that had refused to die down for the rest of the three-hour movie. She'd saved her pocket money and bought postcards and posters with Ms Dixit posing in a hundred different outfits, flashing her toothpaste-commercial pearlies at all and sundry.

Her parents had been relieved. No posters of shirtless Bollywood heroes for their daughter, thank god. She was a decent girl, a good girl. Who was bursting to the seams with secrets she couldn't tell a soul. She could feel them inside her, wriggling like maggots, crawling all over, just there, right under the skin. She started clawing at her veins. She'd be sitting in a lecture on mechanics, and her bench partner would give her a weird look and she'd realize that she'd been raking her own wrist continuously, unconsciously till the skin turned red. And still the secrets stayed inside her.

Then one day, she replaced her nails with a razor blade.

The blood streamed out, surprisingly fast and as she held her wrist under the tap, she felt the pressure ease, just a little bit. As if a festering wound had been drained. It became a ritual for her then. The sharp, painless slice, the gush of red, and the feeling of blessed relief. Soon, her wrists were covered by a tattoo of scarlet scars, which faded to white and shone faintly against her dusky skin. She started wearing full-sleeved tops and shirts so that nobody would notice them. Nobody did. But then, it's difficult to notice somebody's wrists if the somebody never hung out with you. And Laxmi never did. Home–college–home. That was her life now. She had no friends apart from Aisha. No social life except her visits to Aisha's house. No desire for anything except the moments she spent in the bathroom, trying to siphon the secrets hidden in her veins. Days passed, then months. Seasons changed, but to her, every day rose just as grey as the one before.

Till the day it all changed.

She'd gone over to Aisha's house after college, supposedly to finish her physics journal, but really to watch MTV, hoping they'd play Madonna's Erotic *video. It was July and it had rained for days together. All her beloved shirts with their long sleeves, were hanging outside their house, waiting futilely to dry. So she'd been forced to wear a regular half-sleeved t-shirt. To hide her wrists, she'd worn a watch with a thick strap on one hand and a thick bracelet on the other. It was a pretty little thing, the bracelet, delicate-looking and elegant with rows and rows of tiny pearls. Aisha had held up her hand to admire it and the treacherous strands had slipped, revealing the fine network of scars underneath. Aisha had looked horror-struck and she'd been so ashamed of herself then. She'd refused to answer any of Aisha's questions at first, but when the girl had pressed on, she'd broken down and confessed.*

Yes, she was a bad person. A stupid girl, afraid of a silly colour, a shame to her parents, someone to be mocked and despised and left friendless. And worse, she was ... no, she couldn't put it into words. It was unnatural and dirty and abnormal. Yes, that was the word. She was abnormal!

Aisha had stared at her while she said all this. And then, without saying a word, she had hugged her tight. They'd just sat there, in each other's arms, for what felt like ages. When they broke apart, she'd seen the tears on Aisha's cheeks. Her friend had held her face in her hands and slowly, clearly told her that she loved her. Not just as a friend, but as a lost part of her soul. Apparently, she had felt this way for a while, but had been too scared to say anything. 'You don't need to feel the same way about me,' Aisha had said, 'but you need to stop hurting yourself. There is nothing wrong with you. You're perfect. How can you not see that?'

It was as if she had been holding her breath her entire life and she had just been told it was okay to exhale. She threw away the blade that night. She didn't need it anymore. She had something infinitely better: someone who accepted her and loved her, without expectation. And over the next few weeks, she felt her own bullied heart respond to the warmth and love Aisha showered on her. Shyly at first, and then, when her awkward feelings were greeted with enthusiasm, with more confidence, she delved deeper into this unfamiliar yet enchanting new adventure. It didn't seem wrong. It felt ... wonderful.

Days turned to months. Months turned to years. Around her, friends found lovers, and then, in what seemed like hardly any time at all, lost them to others and found new ones for themselves. But Aisha stayed. Their relationship blossomed as they discovered more about each other, things they never knew as friends. She told Aisha about the time a cousin had tried to play doctor with her, only to have his hair pulled till he screamed. Aisha had told her how her father had actually wanted a second son instead of a daughter, and how all her life she had tried not to disappoint him a second time. They spend hours just lying together talking, caressing each other's hands. And then one day, mere hands didn't feel enough. She'd heard that the first time wasn't that great for most women. Hers had been ... indescribably lovely. There was no stopping after that. And why should it have stopped? Everything was perfect.

Till that dark day, two months ago, when Amma had gone to visit her sister. Laxmi'd called Aisha over, confident that Appa wouldn't be home before evening. Except he had come home for some reason and found her and Aisha together, cuddling and kissing on the bed.

She had never thought him capable of saying the things he did. She had seen him angry before, but never in the grasp of a fury like this. He was beyond reason, beyond explanations. And there was nobody to calm him, not even Amma with her well-meaning, but eventually futile murmurs. He warned her to not tell her mother, threatened her, told her to never indulge in such filthy, sinful behaviour again or else he'd take her to someone who'd beat it out of her, someone who would cure her of this abnormal tendency using any means possible. She'd argued and cried, but he had silenced her with a ringing slap across the face.

'If you don't forget about this ... this ... sick nonsense, you will be dead to me, do you understand? It would be better to have a dead daughter than one who brings this kind of shame to my family!'

She had looked mutely at him, tears exhausted, heart sore, and nodded. How could she not? Obedience was a habit that was ingrained in her since she was a child. But it was different now. She wasn't a child anymore. And she wasn't alone either. She didn't have to take this. She didn't have to be bullied into doing anything she didn't want to do.

When she told Aisha her plan to elope, she'd tried to convince her against it. 'Be reasonable, Mimi,' she'd said. 'He'll know whom you've run away to. He'll rage and rave and make your mom cry and she'll call you and cry to you. Do you want to go through all that? They'll go to the police. He'll find you, whatever it takes. He won't put up with the shame of a daughter who has run away from home. I'm with you, whatever you decide, but think it through first. Please.'

And she'd thought, they won't try to find me, if they think I'm beyond finding. He'd have preferred a dead daughter, he'd said. Well, she'd give him one.

They'd called Shweta the next day and told her the plan.

Nineteen

The sky was fading from black to deep purple outside. A few chirps from the proverbial early birds could be heard. Inside, silence reigned. At some point in the last half an hour, Dhruv and Aisha had finished their spat and were now sitting on opposing ends of the couch, fuming. Laxmi planted herself next to Aisha, rubbing her shoulder in a conciliatory way. All three were looking at Avantika, as if waiting for her to say something.

She didn't know what to say. Should she feel sorry for Laxmi? She'd been through hell, for sure. But did that justify the hell she was putting her parents through? And why was she, Avantika, in any place to judge any of them? About Aisha, her feelings were less vague. Yes, she'd been desperate, but to even consider, let alone actually go ahead with, contacting a killer...

She could cry 'misunderstanding' all she wanted, but Avantika couldn't bring herself to forgive her, her intentions and motivations notwithstanding. She could've *died*. And while poets and romantic teenagers might consider love a noble enough cause to die for, she certainly didn't believe in kicking the bucket, that too as an extra in someone else's love story. She'd always felt Mercutio was a bit of a twit, in that respect.

'I'd like to go home now,' she said, looking at Dhruv.

He looked at Aisha, but she was gaping at Avantika.

'That's it? That's all you've got to say?' she asked, eyebrows raised.

'It doesn't matter what she says,' Laxmi said, 'all that matters is whether she will tell anyone.'

Good point, Avantika thought. It was a pretty insane story. A scoop, as the tabloids would put it. But what would she achieve by going public with it? Realistically, she didn't have any solid proof, just a bunch of verbal confessions, which could be denied easily. And then, there was her hate-hate relationship with Aisha. That would take away any credibility she might've had as a neutral commentator. And then, she thought with a sudden stab of guilt, there was the question of whether she'd ever want to wilfully screw up a friend's life. If you could call her that. No, there was only one option left to her.

'Well?' Aisha demanded, 'are you?'

'Depends,' Avantika said.

'*Depends?* On what?'

'Tell me why you sent that man after me. I want to hear it from you. No drama, no attitude. Just ... the truth.'

'That's it?'

'Yep.'

Aisha looked at her suspiciously, then turned to Dhruv and Laxmi, who nodded. Aisha gave a resigned sigh.

'It's ... well ... it's...' she faltered.

'Yes?'

'What do you want me to say?' Aisha asked, shoulders slumped. 'I have only ever loved one person my whole life. She means everything to me. And there was a very real possibility that she would be separated from me. Isn't that enough? Isn't that enough to drive someone to do something stupid, something desperate?'

When Avantika didn't reply, she continued. Her voice was almost plaintive now.

'I didn't ... I never wanted you dead. I just wanted you out of the picture for some time. A week or two till everything got sorted.' She stole a look at Laxmi. 'We're going to the U.S. next week. San Francisco. Same sex marriage is legal there. We'll get married and settle down. I want to be with her for the rest of my life and I don't want some fucking politician with stone-age thinking to tell me if I can or not!'

Avantika looked from Aisha to Laxmi. There were tears in Laxmi's eyes, but Aisha looked resolute, her chin sticking out, the familiar arrogant expression back on her face. She looked like a woman who meant every word she'd just said and Avantika believed she could easily do what she meant to do. This was an unstoppable woman. She could imagine her walking into the morgue, imperious and grief-stricken in turn, pleading, cajoling, threatening, commanding till people bent to her will. If she could pay a killer without batting an eyelid, how difficult was it for her to bribe a couple of cops so they'd forget about the paperwork?

'Must be nice, not having to worry about money,' she muttered.

If Aisha heard her, it didn't show. 'I should've been more specific with my instructions to Manek and I'm really,

really sorry you got hurt,' she said, and this time Avantika could almost make out the sincerity in her voice, 'but I'm not sorry about anything else. If that makes me a bitch, well ... ', she shrugged.

'It *does* make you a bitch,' Avantika said. 'It's one thing crossing a line for love. It's a whole different ball game attempting murder for it.'

She stood up. 'I wish I could wish you well. I do, but I can't. All I can do is promise not to print any of it.'

'Thank you.'

'I'm not doing this for you.'

'Thank you, Avanti,' Laxmi said, squeezing Aisha's hand, 'This means so m—'

'Or you.'

She picked up her backpack and pulled out Laxmi's diary from it. Handing it to the surprised woman, she said, 'Sorry I read some of it. In my defence, I thought you were dead.'

As Laxmi and Aisha turned the pages together, identical smiles on their lips, Avantika turned to Dhruv and raised her eyebrows. 'Well?', she said, 'are you going to take me away from all this or what?'

The BMW pulled out of the driveway and sped towards the Pune–Mumbai Expressway. Behind them, the first rays of the sun peeped over the hills. Deep purple clouds mottled the skies, clashing vividly against the orange-rimmed outlines of the hills. It was quite a stunning view. Avantika looked out of the window of the front seat and stared at nothing.

Aisha had won. Again. She was going to get away with almost-murder and there was nothing anyone could do about it. She had done it for love, she'd said, as if it was something that was supposed to make people nod sagely and go, 'Ah, for love, is it? That's all right then.'

Love, Avantika thought bitterly. It was almost as bad as religion. People gave and took lives for it that weren't theirs to take in the first place. They lied, cheated, used and abused others for love's sake. And you were supposed to understand and get on with life because, hey, it's love after all.

Before leaving, she'd asked Aisha and Laxmi a question that had bothered her for some time.

'Whose body was it? The one y'all burned?'

The two women had looked at her as if she was nuts. Then Laxmi had shrugged casually in the universal 'who-knows' gesture and Aisha, with her usual air of condescension had replied, 'It was just a body, who knows?'

That irritated her. She had tons of things to be really annoyed about today, but this one was rapidly rising to the top of the pile. They may call it the city of dreams, but Mumbai was a hard place. A land with edges of flint, against which the brittle and the fragile broke, like so many shards of glass. But for someone to die unreported, unclaimed and then be *used* in this manner—

She must've been someone's daughter, perhaps someone's sister or wife or mother. She must've meant something to *someone*. And that someone would never know what happened to her. She'd just be one missing person among the hundreds that fall through the cracks of Mumbai every day, never to be seen or heard from again.

She shuddered and rubbed her arms unconsciously.

'Should I turn down the AC?' Dhruv asked.

'No, it's fine.'

She glanced at him sideways. There were shadows under his eyes and the beginnings of a salt-and-pepper stubble along his jawline. What would've made a lesser man look like an escaped convict, made this one look like a Mills and Boons hero. Some killer genes this family has, she thought and smiled wryly to herself.

She'd seen a different side of him last night, a side she was still trying to process. They'd barely spoken after leaving the bungalow, and he didn't seem to mind much. Perhaps the night's revelations had exhausted his quota for conversation. It certainly had exhausted hers. But inner monologues, on the other hand, seemed to be there for the asking, and so hers went on, taking a small moment to remind her that the only time she'd actually gone out of town with an absolutely ravishing man, was to discover that his sister had taken out a contract on her life.

She had just about finished asking her mind to zip it, when her phone pinged. And pinged again. And again. And again. It was a string of Whatsapp messages from Uday, each with a growing sense of panic, till the final one, which was typed out in all caps and urged her to call him, before he called the police. She pressed 'dial' immediately.

'Hello?'

'Thank God! Are you okay? I couldn't get through! Why didn't—'

'Uday, Uday, Uday ... I'm fine. I'm on my way back—'

'From where? I've been messaging you all night, why didn't you reply?'

He wasn't yelling, but in the air-conditioned soundlessness of the car, he may as well have been. 'I didn't get any of the messages, I think the network must've been crap—'

After a few well-chosen words about telecom companies, Uday seemed to calm down. She could imagine him pacing the room, running his hand through his hair, forcing himself to be cool. 'Okay, so I'm just going to wait here at your place till you get back, yes?'

'No, listen, why don't you head home and get some sleep? Or sleep at my place, whatever—'

He told her he'd crash at her place for the night and hung up. She did likewise, only to look up from her phone and see an amused smile on Dhruv's face.

'What?'

'Nothing.'

'You smile creepily for nothing, do you?'

He shrugged, still smiling in that irritating fashion. 'I could stop if you like.'

'How accommodating of you. Now only if you accept that a lot of crap would've been avoided if you'd opened your mouth at the right time—'

He frowned. 'You don't ... let up, do you?'

He gave her a quick look and turned his eyes back on the road. 'Okay, let's go with that. Maybe I should've said something when I saw Manek—'

'*Maybe*?'

'Fine, definitely. I should've told you what I suspected right then. But tell me this, would you have believed me?'

Avantika blinked. Would she have? It was a bit of a stretch, believing that an ex-classmate, even one who'd been as vile as Aisha, would actually pay someone to kill you. And Dhruv was Aisha's brother. She'd have wondered why he was telling her instead of covering up for his sister. Come to think of it, why *had* he bothered to go through the trouble of taking her to Lonavala (or possibly Khandala) and spilling the beans? A strong sense of right and wrong?

If Aisha was to be believed ... but no, that was daft. Maybe he was just scared of what it'd do to his family's reputation if she found out from someone else. But how could he have been sure that she wouldn't want to make the whole affair public? She had no idea. So she asked him.

He pursed his lips. Then, with the air of someone saying something they really didn't want to, he replied, 'All my life, I've tried not to be like Dad. He was a good man in many ways. But I was scared I'd turn out like him with the ... you know. If Manek had succeeded, it'd mean that Aisha had stepped into his shoes and I really didn't want murder to run in the family. I had to make her accountable to *someone*. She had to be pulled up and made to answer, if not to the cops, then to us.'

'But you didn't need me. You could've thrown your elder brother weight a bit and—'

'Yes, but I thought you'd want to know that Laxmi was fine, see it for yourself.'

She still wasn't convinced and he must've sensed that because he added in a softer voice, 'I also wanted you to know that I wasn't involved. That I'd never wish you harm.'

She gulped. There was something in his voice—

'Wasn't it a bit of a risk? What if I'd decided to go to the cops even after hearing the whole thing?'

His face turned grim. 'You have every right to,' he said. 'I guess I just hoped you'd be ... kind. And you are.'

She looked out of the window again. Kind, yes. Kind of a sap. She tried to not feel bad about it and failed. Was she just like everyone else? A sucker for a good sob-story, especially one that involved the L word. Well, at least she wasn't totally deranged when it came to relationships. She'd never go to the lengths Aisha and Laxmi did, just to be with someone. She had more spine than that, she hoped. If push came to shove, she'd stand and fight, instead of running away and playing dead. But then again, who really knew how one would react in a corner? She clicked her tongue in exasperation. Thinking. What a perfectly good waste of brain cells.

'Something wrong?' Dhruv asked.

'No ... well, actually, there's something I've been meaning to ask you about.'

'Oh good. More questions.'

'There was a rumour in school back then, that you and Laxmi were ... you know, dating or whatever.' She looked closely at his face. 'I'm guessing it wasn't true?'

'Obviously not. But I can see why people thought that. She used to be at our place an awful lot. We used to hang out so we were quite comfortable around each other. I think the other girls noticed that, Shweta and Mahira. Laxmi and I would be talking casually and they'd stand in the corner, whispering and giggling. I think they thought there was only one way a girl could be that friendly with a boy.'

Avantika rolled her eyes. Typical. But sadly, not unexpected. Not feeling entirely at home around the opposite sex came with the territory of being a girl in a girl's school. Boys were a strange new species, unknown and exciting. You didn't know what to do about them. What if they sprouted horns or something when provoked? You had to watch from a distance and proceed with extreme caution. Unless over time, you established some kind of relationship with one of them, through non-aggressive body language and small offerings of food[1]. Only then perhaps, were you privy to the secret workings of the male mind[2] and could afford to let your guard down. Hah.

She let out an unexpected yawn.

'You can sleep a bit, if you like,' Dhruv said, 'I won't take advantage of you or anything.'

She grinned, 'I don't see how you could, with your hands on the wheel.'

He gave her a look then and it made her toes curl. 'Are you saying I *could*, when my hands are off the wheel?'

Her mouth dropped open and she looked away to hide her confusion. How had that happened? Dhruv was smiling. He seemed to be enjoying himself.

'Relax,' he said, 'I wouldn't do that. Despite the temptation.'

She cleared her throat, to get over the moment. Funny things were happening in her stomach.

---

1 This remains an effective tactic well into adulthood. Ask anyone who's tried pizza and giggling.

2 A common misconception. Nobody is *ever* privy to the workings of the male mind. If someone is, perhaps they could explain the success of WWE to womankind. Large men in tights pretending to hit each other for the benefit of a paid audience? Kind of a biggie.

'Besides, I think your ... friend ... Uday, is it? He'd have something to say on the subject, if I did.'

'I told you, he's not—'

'I'm sure you think that. But I've been friends with women. You don't stay up the whole night waiting for some girl to come back from wherever, no matter how great a friend you are of hers.'

'You mean *you* don't stay up the whole night—'

'Not just me. The kind of ... concern ... this guy seems to have for you? It can only mean one of two things.'

'Really?' she asked, eyes narrowed.

'Yup. Either you're eighteen and he's your dad, or ... at least as far as he's concerned, you're a lot more than just a friend.'

Twenty

'... and then, we went to Khar Social, but it was packed *obviously*, so I told Storm—that's his actual name, you know, did I mention he's an installation artist?—I said, let's just go to my place and *chill*, but he was like, it's just 1:30, babes, let's do something *fun*, so we—'

Avantika spun around, grabbed Shibani by the shoulders and shook her hard.

'Are you on cocaine?' she yelled. 'Your social life puts Lady Gaga's to shame! Have you no sense of decency at all?'

Of course, all this happened in a matter of moments, deep in the dark corners of her mind. In reality, she turned calmly to her colleague and said, 'That sounds amazing, were there jugglers?'

It was hugely fulfilling to see the puzzled frown on Shibani's face. But she had underestimated the girl. Refusing to be fazed by something she didn't understand, she went on: 'No, but funny you should mention jugglers, because we went to this bar—it doesn't have a name, people just know where it is and show up, cool, na?—and the *bartender*, you won't *believe* this—'

From across the room, Uday held two thumbs up and gave her a happy grin. The bastard. She'd told him everything, of course, and after yelling at her a bit for a variety of things—falling asleep in Dhruv's car, agreeing to keep everything she heard a secret, not even landing a few punches on Aisha's face—he'd agreed that she didn't have any solid proof and couldn't do anything about it.

'I wish I'd recorded that conversation on my phone,' she'd groaned.

'Wouldn't matter, it's inadmissible evidence,' he'd replied.

And that's where the matter would've ended had Dhruv not put his silly assumption in her head. She wanted to ignore it as the stupid surmise of a man, who was, who was ... alright, very nice to look at, but still.

She'd have to talk to Uday about it. But wouldn't that spoil everything? Look at him, sitting there and grinning at her misery. That's what friends did. She'd hate it if this was replaced by some kind of stupid awkwardness. Ugh.

Then, Nathan walked in and called the meeting to order. Avantika quietly watched him hand out the week's assignments. She was determined to be a good girl in this meeting. It was important that she not fuck up. There was a lot hanging in the—

'Pandit,' Nathan said, peering over his glasses. 'You're very quiet today. Here, you can cover this.'

He slid a press release towards her. She took it mutely, and was skimming it when he decided to give her a summary.

'Some celebrity dietician—Megha someone—has a new book coming out, where she's talked about going on an all-fruit diet. Go cover the launch.'

Personally, Avantika thought it was bananas to pick fruit over, say, bacon. But she nodded sagely anyway. Nathan was still looking at her. Now he leaned forward, as if trying to watch her more closely.

'The book's called ... *My Experiments with Fruit*.'

No. *What?* She could hear hysterical laughter in her head. So. Many. Jokes. Avantika sniffed, then cleared her throat. 'Super,' she said, struggling to keep her voice from shaking.

Nathan gave her an odd look. Uday was carefully looking at the ceiling, trying not to laugh.

'Are you sure you heard the name correctly?'

'I did,' she said, drawing a huge breath. 'It sounds ... interesting.'

Nathan nodded, shooting a suspicious glance her way. He was about to move to the next item, when a voice said, 'Er, I had a story idea.'

To Avantika's horror, she realized it was her voice. Nathan was peering at her again, as was the rest of the room. No doubt, they were wondering what fresh pile of dung she was about to step in.

'A story idea?' Nathan asked. 'Could this be the story you were, what was it you called it, yes, "chasing"?' You could almost hear the air-quotes dropping into place.

'Yes,' Avantika said meekly. Then she took a deep breath and said, 'WardboysaredoingautopsiesatBhagwanwadi Hospital.'

There should have been some kind of effect. A respectful hush, perhaps or the loud silence of every pair of ears in a room straining to hear what would be said next. But no, that kind of thing doesn't happen to everyone. So all Avantika got in return were a few half-hearted whats and a suppressed giggle. One person yawned, without even bothering to cover it up. She looked helplessly at Nathan. Surely with his experience, his fervour for journalism, he would've heard and understood what she said. Surely he wouldn't just sit back and say—

'What?' Nathan asked. 'What did you say?'

Avantika slumped back in her seat. Then she leaned forward again.

'I said…' she began.

'Ward boys. Are doing. Post-mortems,' Nathan said slowly. 'Are you sure?'

Avantika nodded furiously. 'I have a source and everything. He was *there*. He's probably done a few himself. He—'

'Can you trust him? Is he reliable?'

Avantika thought of Ganesh, with his tobacco-stained grin and henna-tinted hair. 'Practically a Gandhian,' she said.

After the meeting, she accosted Uday, who greeted her with a high-five.

'Nice going,' he said. 'It's a hell of a story. Let me know if you need any help.'

She nodded, then began fidgeting. This was it. This didn't have to be it, did it? Couldn't she just not ask the question?

No, she had to. It wasn't fair to Uday if he was being nice to her because he ... liked her. It was too much like using a guy and she didn't want to be the kind of woman who did shit like that.

'Do you have to go to the loo?' Uday asked, watching her practically vibrate on the spot.

'No, what? No, I have to ask you something.'

'Okay?'

'Do you ... are you...' she waved her hands vaguely in the air.

'Confused? Little bit, yeah.'

'No. Idiot.'

Then she lowered her voice and looked around. They were standing in the balcony outside the office, which was usually colonized by smokers. Today, blessedly, there wasn't a single soul around.

'Look,' she said. 'Do you have ... feelings for me or something?' She made a face.

For a moment, Uday was absolutely silent. Then he looked at the ceiling. 'Yeah. Kind of.'

'*Kind of*?'

'Well, I have feelings of ...' he looked into the distance, as if seeking inspiration or perhaps just the right word, 'exasperation? Amusement? Sometimes even a bit of violence. Nothing serious, you understand, just a tap across the head when you're being an ass—'

She punched his arm. Nothing happened. She punched it again. This time, her knuckles twinged a bit. She massaged them with a frown.

'I did mention I go to the gym, you know,' Uday said reproachfully.

'Whatever,' she said, drawing herself up. 'Bloody Dhruv Juneja, saying things—'

'You called?' said a voice nearby and of course, it was Dhruv, dapper as usual, familiar smirk firmly in place.

She rolled her eyes. 'Tell me the truth,' she said and he raised his eyebrows, 'Can you teleport? Is it a superpower they hand out with BMWs in case the car breaks down? Because you're always popping up without warning.'

He was holding a large brown paper bag before him. Its handles were made from a navy blue satin ribbon. You didn't have to reach the contents of the bag to see that this was going to be an expensive exercise. He held the bag out to her.

'Like all good things in life,' he grinned.

She took the bag and reached into it, shooting suspicious looks at Dhruv the whole time. She wasn't the only one—Uday was sizing up Dhruv as well, giving him a stony-faced look for good measure. Under a layer of tissue paper, her fingers touched smooth leather. She pulled away the last of the wrapping. It was a purse.

To be precise, a messenger bag made from rich brown leather, with dull brass fastenings. On the handle, hand-stitched in dull gold thread, were an A and J, capital, serif, interlocked. Yet it was nothing like Aisha's other colourful creations. It was a working woman's bag, and wouldn't have made it through the door of a high-tea or a kitty party. It was made for rough handling, ups and downs, dropping and picking up and stuffing with the kind of things that makes a woman's handbag such a mysterious object for men. It seemed made for her. And yet—'I'm sorry, I can't accept it,' she said, handing it back to Dhruv.

'You don't like it?' he asked, genuinely surprised.

'No, it's lovely, it's perfect,' she said, eyeing it longingly, 'but ... it's too much like a bribe.'

'No, no,' he said. 'Don't misunderstand me. This isn't some kind of ... thing to keep your mouth shut—'

'But if it's from Laxmi and Aisha, then—'

'Them? Hah,' said Dhruv, 'It's from ... me. Think of it as a sorry-my-stupid-sister-tried-to-kill-you gift.'

Avantika shot him a sharp look and he wilted a bit.

'Too soon?'

'Yes. And stupid isn't the word I'd use.'

'Probably not,' he agreed, 'self-centred may be more accurate. But that's what love does to people, I guess.'

Avantika strangled the urge to correct him. Love, real love, she wanted to say, is about thinking about someone else to the extent that you put yourself in second place. Mothers understood this instinctively. The rest of us, she felt, plod along trying to pretend that we get it, while being laughably clueless the whole time.

On the other hand, a treacherous voice inside her piped up, isn't loving someone and then thinking *only* of them, of protecting *only* that love, to the exclusion of everyone and everything including family, friends, values and country, also a kind of selfishness? She shook her head to clear it. Shakespeare had got it totally wrong, she thought. Perhaps love doesn't make fools, so much as selfish assholes of us all.

'Thanks for the bag,' she said to Dhruv. 'It'll be a nice ... reminder.'

He grinned cheekily. 'Not of me, I hope. I just talked to Nathan and I'm going to be doing a running photo-feature for you guys. You know, parts of Mumbai that rarely get shot. I'm thinking of calling it "Unseen City". What do you think?'

Avantika was about to nod approvingly, when Uday piped up. 'It's a bit ... first thought, don't you think?'

Dhruv looked a little taken aback at this casual rudeness, but he recovered quickly. 'Right, thanks,' he said with a knowing smile to Avantika, 'I guess I needed ...ah ... a *neutral* third person opinion.'

And with a cheery wave, he was gone.

'Arrogant asshole,' Uday muttered to his retreating back. 'I'll give you this, Avanti, at least you have the good taste not to date someone like that.'

Deep inside Avantika's mind, something sat up and went, hmmm.

'Oh, he's not all that bad,' she said, watching Uday's face carefully. 'He was a total gentleman the whole time we were at that bungalow.'

Uday looked stormy for a second, but it passed quickly. 'I'm just glad you're back alive,' he said, giving her an affectionate hug and messing her hair. 'It would've been a bitch covering features till Nathan found someone new.'

Just then, his phone rang and he held up a finger, indicating that he had to take it. Talking rapidly on the handset, he walked away from her. Avantika watched him thoughtfully, as he walked out of the balcony and into the main office. That hug had been ... different. Not entirely platonic. Maybe just a little bit protective. Or was it possessive? She'd have to think about this. But it would have to be later. Right now, she had work to do. She dialled a number on her phone.

'Hello? Ganesh?' she said. 'When does your shift end?'

Acknowledgements

Some books just write themselves. Allegedly. This one didn't. And without the support and somctimes ass-kicking of a few wonderful people, it may never have seen the light of day. So here goes, in no particular order, a vote of thanks:

Vahishta Mistry, you are the best first-draft reader a girl can hope for, all praises and positivity, with just the right way of pointing out glaring inadequacies so that I don't feel like slashing my wrist with a sharp-edged A4 sheet.

Pavitra Jayaraman and Alok Pandey, thank you for entertaining out-of-the-blue phone calls and ridiculous questions regarding your professions. I'd say there won't be more, but why make promises I can't keep?

Ishita Desai, Ahana Chaudhuri, you are jewels among commoners and the most magnificent beta readers this side of Paradise Talkies.

Nishant Pratap, I cannot believe you took the time to read and review this in the first month of your new job. Your multitasking game is very strong, my friend.

A quick shout-out to the girls of the batch of 1997 of a school that shall not be named. Thank you for making high school so educational for me.

To Swati Daftuar, my wonderful editor: thank you for taking a chance on a book so many had turned down and for not changing it much. I'm truly grateful.

Irawati, my love, this book was conceived just weeks after you came into the world, but while I love both of you, you should know you're my favourite. Now if you could just start sleeping on time again, so I can write some more?

And Arjun, you are an exceptionally demanding reader who keeps expecting me to write better, be better, do better. Thank god for that.